ZOË JENNY

THE
POLLEN
ROOM

A NOVEL

TRANSLATED BY ELIZABETH GAFFNEY

SCRIBNER PAPE
PUBLISHED BY SIMON & SCHUSTER
NEW YORK LONDON SYDNEY SINGAPORE

SCRIBNER PAPERBACK FICTION
SIMON & SCHUSTER, INC.
ROCKEFELLER CENTER
1230 AVENUE OF THE AMERICAS
NEW YORK, NY 10020

THIS BOOK IS A WORK OF FICTION. NAMES, CHARACTERS, PLACES,
AND INCIDENTS EITHER ARE PRODUCTS OF THE AUTHOR'S IMAGINATION
OR ARE USED FICTITIOUSLY. ANY RESEMBLANCE TO ACTUAL EVENTS
OR LOCALES OR PERSONS, LIVING OR DEAD, IS ENTIRELY COINCIDENTAL.

COPYRIGHT © 1997 BY FRANKFURTER VERLAGSANSTALT GMBH, FRANKFURT AM MAIN
ENGLISH LANGUAGE TRANSLATION COPYRIGHT © 1999 BY SIMON & SCHUSTER, INC.

ALL RIGHTS RESERVED, INCLUDING THE RIGHT OF REPRODUCTION
IN WHOLE OR IN PART IN ANY FORM.

FIRST SCRIBNER PAPERBACK FICTION EDITION 2000
PUBLISHED BY ARRANGEMENT WITH FRANKFURTER VERLAGSANSTALT GMBH
SCRIBNER PAPERBACK FICTION AND DESIGN ARE TRADEMARKS
OF MACMILLAN LIBRARY REFERENCE USA, INC. USED UNDER LICENSE
BY SIMON & SCHUSTER, THE PUBLISHER OF THIS WORK.

DESIGNED BY KAROLINA HARRIS

MANUFACTURED IN THE UNITED STATES OF AMERICA

10 9 8 7 6 5 4 3 2 1

THE LIBRARY OF CONGRESS HAS CATALOGED THE SIMON & SCHUSTER EDITION
AS FOLLOWS:
JENNY, ZOË.
[BLÜTENSTAUBZIMMER. ENGLISH]
THE POLLEN ROOM : A NOVEL / ZOË JENNY : [TRANSLATED BY ELIZABETH
GAFFNEY].
P.   CM.
I. TITLE.
PT2670.E49B5813   1999
833'.914—DC21   98-47401
CIP

ISBN 0-684-85458-9
0-684-85459-7 (PBK)

ORIGINALLY PUBLISHED IN GERMANY IN 1997 AS *DAS BLÜTENSTAUBZIMMER*

I

WHEN MY mother moved to an apartment a few blocks away, I remained with Father.

The building we lived in smelled of damp stone. During the daytime, my father made books on a printing press in the laundry room. Every afternoon, when I got home from kindergarten, I would go to find him there, and together we climbed the stairs to the apartment and made lunch. In the evening, before I fell asleep, he would stand beside my bed and draw glowing orange pictures in the darkness with his cigarette. Then, after he had brought me a cup of warm milk with honey, he would sit down at the table and begin to write. I drifted off to the rhythms of the typewriter and, if I awakened, I would see the back of his head through the open door, his hair lit up like a bright crown by the table lamp, and the countless cigarette butts that he lined up, one next to the other, on the edge of the table.

No one ever bought the books my father published, and so he took a night job driving a delivery truck so he could afford to continue printing them. At first the books were stacked up in the cellar, then in the attic, and finally all through the house.

At night I would fall into a restless slumber. Fractured dreams floated past my sleeping eyes like scraps of paper in the raging torrent of a river. Then I would hear a clatter and find myself wide awake. I looked up at the spiderwebs on the ceiling and knew that my father was in the kitchen. He had just put the water on to boil. In a little while the whistle shrieked, just for a moment, until he grabbed the kettle off the burner. The smell of coffee reached me in my room as it brewed, hot water dribbling, little by little, through the filter and into the Thermos. Then came a series of muffled rustling noises and a moment of quiet. My breath quickened. A lump rose in my throat and swelled to enormous proportions as I watched my father put on his leather jacket and pull the door quietly closed behind him.

A barely perceptible click.

I hauled myself out from under the covers and leaned against the window. Slowly I counted, one, two, three. He reappeared by the time I reached seven and moved with quick steps across the sidewalk, bathed in the gloomy yellow glow of the street lamp. When I got to ten, he was passing by the restaurant on the corner, and there he turned away, out of sight. I held my breath, and a few seconds later I heard the engine of his delivery truck roar to life, then grow quieter as it traveled away from my window, farther and farther, and finally faded away altogether.

The darkness crept out from every corner like a starving beast. I went to the kitchen, flipped on the light, sat at the table and wrapped my fingers around his coffee cup, empty but still warm. I scanned the rim for brown splotches of dried coffee. If he didn't come back, they would be the last signs I had of his existence, his life. As the cup gradually cooled in my hands, the night pervaded the house completely, spreading into every cranny. I put it down carefully and returned to my room through the narrow hall.

The insect was squatting in front of the window frame through which I had just watched my father go away. It glared at me malevolently. I sat on the farthest corner of the bed without letting the creature out of my sight. At any moment, I feared, it might spring into my face and run across my body on its knobby, quivering legs. In the center of the room, flies wildly orbited the light bulb. I stared into the light, at the flies, but out of the corner of my eye, I watched the black insect lurking motionlessly before the window.

Time and again exhaustion enveloped me like a great warm pelt. I strained myself from beneath half-closed lids to distinguish between individual flies, but they blurred increasingly into a dark band of circular motion hanging in the air. The insect sniggered at me. I sensed that its feelers were inching slowly closer to where my feet hung over the edge of the bed, and I bolted for the kitchen, where I plunged my head under cold running water in the sink.

My bladder was full and tight. It hurt to hold it, but the bathroom was on a landing halfway up the flight of stairs, and I was afraid to go up there because the light in the hallway turned off automatically after just a short time.

I knew that back in my room the insect was beginning to move, planning to attack me as soon as I entered the stairwell. I paced the kitchen, humming snatches of the songs I had learned in kindergarten, but I only knew a few of them by heart, and the songs I pieced together came out differently each time. As the pain from holding my bladder blossomed, so did the volume of my voice. Somehow I hoped this would transport me out of my body entirely. Finally, I squatted in front of the kitchen cabinets and peed into a vase clutched between my thighs.

When the dawn finally glimmered at the kitchen window, the insect retreated to some distant hiding place. The darkness was eaten away by the light, bit by bit, and I returned to my bed exhausted, to burrow beneath the covers. At seven the phone rang. It was father, calling from the road to wake me up.

SOMETIMES THE night remained at bay. The windowpane reflected a sea of heads bobbing and swaying to Mick Jagger. I sat on a woman's lap and helped her guide a bottle with four roses on its label to her lips.

Every time she threw her head back to laugh, liquor escaped from the corners of her mouth and ran in fine lines down her powdered cheeks. She laughed the hardest when Father did one of his wild dances, spinning with his arms flying wide, and tripped over a stack of books. She guffawed at him, and the cool alcohol burst from her lips, spraying me in the face.

"Do you want to hear a secret?" I asked her, pulling the bottle from her face.

"A secret?" she gurgled. She rolled the word around her mouth as if it were a bonbon. "I like secrets." She pressed a kiss onto the cheek of the young man sitting beside her.

"Come on, I'll show you," I said. Her hand lay warm and flaccid in mine as I led her through the maze of books and bottles that cluttered my father's work area. When we got to my room, she plopped down on the bed and put the bottle back to her lips. I brought out my drawings from under the dresser.

"What are those?" She gazed through watery eyes at the black blotches on the sheets of paper.

"It's the insect. It comes at night, when I'm alone, and eats up my sleep."

"Oh, really?" She looked at me. Her brow was furrowed. I took the drawings back and returned them to their hiding place. My back was to her.

"Do you believe in God?" I asked.

But by the time I turned around, she had already collapsed onto the floor, the empty bottle still clutched in her hand. I bent over and gently tried to rouse her. Her body didn't move, but beneath her rosy eyelids I could see her eyes darting back and forth in agitation. Music and noisy laughter came from my father's workroom. I turned off the light. Surely the insect would not dare to show itself in my room that night. And if it came, at least there was that body lying on the floor beside my bed, heavy as stone.

O N E   N I G H T my father had an accident. He fell asleep at the wheel and drove into a tree. He went into shock and lay in bed for two weeks, sick with a fever. I unplugged the telephone and pulled the curtains closed. When the doorbell rang we ignored it. It's just someone wanting money anyway, he said as he wearily rolled over in bed. He reported me sick at kindergarten and warned me not to let anyone see me when I went around the corner for sandwiches and cigarettes. I would slip my arms into the sleeves of the oversized wind-breaker that we'd gotten from a social service agency, along with a lot of other clothes. I pulled the hood over my head and ran the whole way down the street to the market.

DAYLIGHT FILTERED through the yellow curtains, and when it was a nice day outside there would be faint stripes of sun lying across the bedspread.

Those rays have come a long way, said my father, and now they're stopping here with us.

I went to get Nico and Florian, my two best and only friends, and set them down in the light.

I believe they would like to go on a trip, I said.

Nico, a blue pacifier with the rubber worn rag-ged all over from chewing, sat on the right at my father's feet. Florian, a yellow pacifier, was on the left. With one of them in each hand, I bounded over the covers, conquered the valleys and mountains and seas that lay between the folds of fabric, and landed at last at my father's head, a labyrinth of dark hair. We never have to go outside again, I told him. We have everything we need right here, the sun and the mountains, the ocean and the valleys.

I went into the kitchen, and into my bedroom, and drew the curtains there too. From my window I could see the neighborhood children crawling around in the street, rolling brightly colored marbles into the grooves of the cast-iron manhole covers. Play with them, my father always said when I spent entire days in the laundry room, sitting on the dryer and watching the paper be taken up by the rollers and spat out the other side, freshly printed. But I never played with them, just watched them from my window.

The girls giggled maliciously when one of the boys missed a shot and his marble rolled away into the street and down a gutter. In retaliation, the boys pinned the girls on their backs and spat into their faces. When it rained, they vanished all at once through the thick glass door of a building across the street. Its gray façade turned nearly black in the rain, but the windows, lit from within, looked like small, peaceful islands.

That was the only time I thought I would have liked to be with them. I envied them for being inside those squares of light.

•

ONE AFTERNOON I decided to take a boat trip with Nico and Florian. I told father that our boat was just like Sinbad the Sailor's and hauled all the covers and cushions in the whole apartment onto his bed. I made them into a great mountain and sat on top of it. Father was an enormous octopus, and when he wrapped his arms around the mountain of bedclothes, the ship rocked up and down until the raging of the storm capsized it with a crash, and we lay on the floor, covers and cushions strewn wildly about.

The storm had only just abated when the doorbell rang. A woman with strawberry-blond hair teetered up the stairs, into the apartment and vanished into the kitchen with my father.

As I gathered up cushions and covers, the remains of the ship that had been dashed to bits, I could hear her strange, loud voice coming from behind the kitchen door.

SOON AFTERWARD, my father rented her an empty room upstairs. On the floor next to her mattress, she kept books with stars in them. Her fingers would glide over the shiny black pages.

Here is the Great Bear, and here is Draco, she said to me, but I didn't see bears or dragons, just white spots strewn across a dark ground. When she wasn't sitting in the lotus position on her mattress with her eyes closed, she was in the kitchen smoking cigarettes with different men and shrieking. Eliane didn't laugh, she shrieked, and it made her face turn red. I detested her when she sat in the kitchen, and I detested the men she sat with too. They pulled me over to them and tousled my long hair.

"Just like a big pile of spaghetti," they said, grinning.

"Leave my hair alone, asshole," I snarled and tore myself away.

"Where'd she ever learn *that* word?" they pretended to wonder and roared with laughter when Eliane blushed. I much preferred to see her sitting on the mattress in her room.

"When you meditate," she told me, "you forget everything around you. You don't think about anything at all."

"But do you still remember your own name?"

"Nope. You forget everything, absolutely everything, even where you are."

"But where are you, then?"

"Nowhere," she said, earnestly.

"But what's there, there?"

"Everyone has to find that out on their own."

When I came to the door, she looked like a statue. Her cheeks, which were usually so ruddy, seemed pale and waxy. Her mouth was closed, like a fortress I had good reason to be afraid of approaching. But her nervous, flickering eyelashes betrayed her. I held my hand under her nose and felt the hesitation of her breath on the back of my hand, her fear.

"I know that you know that I'm here," I said.

Her eyes flew open, her mouth contracted into a tight dark hole, and she reached out and boxed my ears. She pushed me out the door, and from then on her room was off limits to me.

After my father finally married her, Eliane sat in the kitchen more often. I watched her peel oranges, smoke cigarettes, eat mountains of nuts. The piles of nutshells on the table grew higher and higher, and crowding in between them were glasses and huge overflowing ashtrays. Now and then one of the ashtrays would wind up in my father's studio. Eliane would spin her strawberry-blond head around in circles searching for it. And when she didn't find it, she would stamp through the apartment screaming and yelling.

After one of these attacks, as Father always referred to her bouts of rage, he gave her a pocket video game as a present. It was like a fireman had burst into a burning building with a hose and skillfully extinguished a blaze in the rafters. After that, Eliane would sit quietly in the kitchen for hours on end, playing her game. I forgot about her, and at some point she simply went away. She left behind a pair of panties with tiny blue flowers on them and a dried-up underarm deodorant stick that I found when I was wiping up under the kitchen cabinets. A year later, a card arrived. A picture of a white sand beach and a swaying palm tree.

Greetings from sunny Spain.
—Eliane

I wondered if she now sat in the lotus position under that palm tree and tried to imagine that she wasn't there.

S U N D A Y S   I   always spent with my mother. In the evening she would stand in front of the big mirror with her hair up in rollers and dab at her face with pencils and little sponges. I handed her the tubes and bottles that lay on the windowsill and unscrewed fancy caps in the shapes of flowers and teardrops from perfume bottles. As soon as the babysitter came, she let her hair down, and it fanned out, brown and sweet smelling, across her back. Then she was gone.

Later on, her whimpering would rouse me, and I felt my way through the darkness to her bed. She lay under the brightly flowered coverlet, trembling with some secret pain that I could not understand. Only a fragment of her face was visible —the triangle of her nose and mouth—the rest hidden by her white hands. After a while she threw back the covers and I crawled inside the salty-warm bed.

ONCE A week she also picked me up from school. From far away I could see her standing beside the iron gate, and I ran to her from across the schoolyard. She took me by the hand, and together we set out for the city.

In the dressing rooms, which smelled of sweat and plastic, she would fold up a few items and pack them into her great shoulder bag. The rest she returned to the shelves. At the counter she would pay for a pair of socks or a T-shirt and stroke my hair as if I were a newborn kitten. When we walked away, the saleswomen watched us through the plate-glass windows, clasping their hands with pleasure. On those days, there was no limit to the number of slices of chocolate cake that I was allowed to eat, and my mother was soft and happy. Afterward, in the restaurant, I slurped syrupy drinks through a straw and my mother reached into the depths of her bag to touch the new fabric, her lips slightly open, her eyes huge, as if she couldn't believe what she'd gotten away with. She was happy. Back at her apartment, she would snip the price tags from the clothes, hang them up on her wheeled clothes rack and roll it into her room with her head held high like a queen.

I continued to wait for her at the iron gate when school let out, but she didn't come. When I asked Father if something had happened, he only shook his head in silence. A few weeks later, she turned up again, kissed me on the head, and told me to get into the car. This time we didn't go into the city, and I was glad. She parked at the head of a nature trail through the woods. I leapt over deep treadmarks in the trail that had been gouged into the hot, dry earth by a tractor. My mother's bright dress billowed around her body like a cloud. I knew she had something important to tell me. She didn't speak though, the whole way, until the tractor tracks had faded away and we were standing in an open field.

My mother lay down on the brittle grass and I beside her. I could feel the pounding of the pulse in her smooth neck, so close. She said she had met a man, Alois, and that she loved him as she once had loved my father. She was going to go away with him, for good. Everywhere I looked I saw red and yellow flowers. Their perfume filled the air, making me giddy and tired. I turned on my side and pressed my ear to the earth. I watched her mouth as she talked on, but all I heard was a humming and a rustling, as if something were moving deep within the earth.

I looked at her. She gazed toward the sky. The humming sound rose above us and hovered there palpably, like a blue veil.

II

EXCEPT FOR a couple of emaciated cats
stalking around in the garbage and hissing at each
other, the alleyways are empty at lunchtime. A
warm wind carries the stink of piss through the
rows of houses, where it mingles with the odors of
tomato sauce and disinfectant that waft from open
kitchen windows. Plates clatter as they're banged
down on tables, and the voice of a child drifts from
a doorway.

Behind the bank there is a park where, most
days, mothers sit with their Thermos bottles and
sandwiches and watch their children playing in the
sandbox. Today the park is empty, but I walk over
to the music pavilion just as I always do. Music is
never actually played there, not even on Sundays—
it's all boarded up. I sit down on a bench to wait
until it's time to pick Lucy up.

Every Monday we take the bus into the city
and I accompany Lucy to Dr. Alberti's. Then I come
here to wait out the fifty-minute therapeutic hour.
It's much too short, Lucy once complained—she's
only just getting started by the time three quarters
of an hour have passed. I always try to imagine
what Lucy says to Dr. Alberti, once she gets started,

but all I can picture is her sitting there, arms dangling over the arms of the chair, staring at the blank wall with her mouth closed, neither yielding nor resisting, clamped tight like an oyster.

Or does she tell him everything and me nothing?

Perhaps she explains every detail of her thoughts to Dr. Alberti, who is probably a small, fat man with thick tufts of black hair on the backs of his hands. He is a man who has had his name and title carved into a brass plaque, a man who calls himself a healer of souls. I laughed the first time I heard Lucy use that phrase, and asked her if one could actually heal a soul as if it were a broken leg.

A COUPLE of skateboarders cruise through the park, their long T-shirts flapping around their knees as they hug the curve around the pavilion. Two girls with yellow nylon knapsacks sit down on a bench near me, take out a video game and start to play. The little plastic box emits beeps and explosions, and the girl playing bites her lower lip in concentration. The other one stares at the screen excitedly, yelling, "Now! Now! Shoot already! Shoot!"

Dr. Alberti's office is in the old part of the city, near the boarded-up church. Lucy says they're renovating it. Struts of metal scaffolding shine in the sun and the bandaged body of the church rises like a mummy over the wide front stairs. Kids hang out on the steps, eating, sleeping, looking passively out onto the square.

I go past pricey shops and a bank to an escalator that delivers me into the subterranean city. The ring with its heavy traffic divides the city into two parts and the subterranean city serves as an underpass between them. Not long ago, ancient skeletons were found down here, and since then it's become a tourist attraction.

I speed through the narrow, dim passages. It smells like cold stone and is always damp, even in high summer. Behind a pane of glass set into the earth, one of the skeletons is on display. The skull, the pelvis and splinters of the shinbone have been carefully arranged. An information card says they are the bones of an eight-year-old boy. Tourists stand in a little cluster around the railing and whisper.

In the dimmer niches of the underground city, small groups of addicts gather. They light candles so they can see to find their veins more easily. Every now and then you catch sight of their emaciated faces in the flickering light or come across a block of stone studded with candle stumps that have been overlooked by the clean-up crews who patrol this place at night.

A barely perceptible pounding throbs through the underground city at all times—excavations never cease.

A T T H E far end of the passage, the escalator brings me back up to the surface. The glare and heat blast me in the face so powerfully that, just for a moment, I want to go back down.

When the stairs flatten out at the top, the first thing I see is the equestrian monument. It seems strange and implausible standing there beside a street so densely traveled by cars. Behind it the chimneys and apartment buildings jut into the blue sky. A young woman is sitting in front of the monument playing the cello, but her music is audible only when the traffic light turns red and all the cars come to a stop. She's wearing blue sweatpants and black lace-up boots, and her bleached-blond hair is sloppily pinned up. Half her face is hidden behind enormous orange-lensed sunglasses.

I saw her the last time I was here, and the time before that, and the time before that. In fact, I've seen her here every single time I've been by. She doesn't seem to have anything else to do. Her image stays with me the whole way to Dr. Alberti's. When I get there, I pace the sidewalk in front of his office anxiously. It always seems as if I haven't seen Lucy in a long, long time, because no matter how hard I try, I cannot remember her face. She comes through the door at last, and we greet each other with terse, awkward gestures. We walk to the restaurant silently, side by side.

The big, mirrored dining room is never full. An older couple sits together with their dog at their feet. Three men at another table look up at us as we enter, then resume their conversation as soon as we sit down. Lucy's hair is brushed back and gathered into a knot. She lights a cigarette and blows the smoke off to one side.

"That was it," she says. "I'm not going back to him. I don't need him anymore."

"So, you're feeling better then?"

"Yes, goddammit. I'm feeling better. You know, I don't want your pity, Jo. I've never needed your pity."

"It's not that I pity you, but this last time around was pretty bad. I don't want you to hurt yourself."

When the waitress comes to the table with menus, Lucy pushes hers to the side and leans forward over the table.

"You were afraid I was going to kill myself."

I nod. Lucy's head tips back and she begins to laugh. A man at the next table looks over and stares at her. She leans toward me again.

"My dear Jo," she says. "A few months ago, I

came very close to dying unwillingly. Why would I choose to die after making it through that alive? You've got some crazy ideas, Jo."

She picks up the menu and flips the pages.

The face of the waitress who flits from table to table is the same shade of faded pink as her uniform, the tablecloths, the walls and the carpet, all except for a half-moon-shaped patch around the entranceway, where the pink is stained a dirty brown.

The man who noticed Lucy laughing is speaking loudly. I see from her face that she's trying to eavesdrop, but his words are obscured by the whirring of the air conditioner. When the waitress stoops over to pick up a fallen napkin, the man's eyes meet Lucy's over her back. I am in the middle of telling her about some splendid flowers I've seen in a shop window, but she doesn't hear a word I'm saying. Then, suddenly, she pushes her plate to the side and announces that she won't be coming home with me after we eat. She's going into the city. Today is a special day for her, she tells me. She's told Alberti everything. She has finally accepted that Alois is dead. She's finished with that for once and for all.

I leave the restaurant with the sensation that I have been betrayed.

Lucy is a liar. These four words rise up before me like bubbles coming to the surface. They vanish and reappear until, at last, they begin to be intelligible to me, to stand firmly in my mind. Dr. Alberti doesn't know a thing. Lucy has lied to him session after session. Now she's convinced herself that her own lies are true and she doesn't need him anymore.

It's as if I have been granted a momentary glimpse of a messy room whose occupant has forgotten to close the door. But the fact that Lucy has been lying does not alienate me from her. On the contrary, it seems to place her more firmly in my grasp. I've been trying to get *some* sort of hold on her since I arrived here a year ago.

At the bus stop, I see the old couple from the restaurant, waiting. They're talking to their little black dog, who sits before them panting, tortured by the heat. When the bus comes, they lean against each other for support as they climb aboard, muttering words of mutual encouragement. As they ascend the first step, their feet dangle precipitously in the air, and when they finally reach it, they stop there and rest for a while. I feel like giving them a shove to hurry things along, but instead I just look at their wispy white hair and breathe in the sour smell of their old age. I can't stand old people. I get on after them and sit down by the window, as far away from them as possible.

I have never before made the trip to Lucy's house from the city alone. It's still just a couple of weeks since I managed to drag her out of the pollen room. Sometimes at night I'm awakened by noises outside my window and I see Lucy walking through the garden in the quiet dawn light, taking the heads of flowers between her fingers and breathing in their scent. She uses her fingernails to pluck the thin, fragile stamens from amongst the petals and collects them in her hand. Then she goes to the pollen room and scatters the dust on the floor. Pollen is everywhere, covering the floor and the sill of the high basement windows. A mattress covered with a sheet, the only object in the room, lies on the floor between the cellar's two columns. This is the mattress she lay on after Alois died.

The morning after the burial, I watched from the dining room window as a garbage truck pulled up. Lucy and a couple of workers threw everything that had belonged to Alois into the maw of the truck. One of the men took an ax and hacked up the paintings that were too large to fit. As soon as the men had gone, Lucy left the house and didn't return until late at night. She was carrying a basket of freshly picked flowers—just the heads. For several days she refused to answer my questions or to speak at all. She left the house in the morning and returned at night with flowers. When she had totally covered the floor of Alois's studio with pollen, she closed the door behind her and locked herself in. Alois had installed a small, round window in the heavy steel door so that Lucy could see whether he was painting or just lounging in the hammock that he'd strung up between the columns. Only if he was in the hammock was she allowed to go in and see him.

I called to Lucy again and again through that little Plexiglas window. At first I waved my arms in the air, trying to get her attention, but she never looked my way. I tried to coax her out with every imaginable suggestion: At first outings, then trips abroad, and finally I offered her a round-the-world tour. I sketched out our route and held the paper up to the window so she could think it over. The next morning I called in to her: "So, are we going?"

She didn't stir. I kicked the door, but it didn't budge, even when I hurled myself against it, cursing. I peered through the little window, but the pile of flesh that was my mother just continued to lie there, mute. The only sign of life was the minute, barely visible rise and fall of her body as she breathed. I begged her at least to give me some indication that she heard me. She didn't stir. I threatened to call a psychiatric hospital, have her committed and then burn the house down. No response. She lay quiet and motionless with her face pressed into the mattress. I ran around to the garden in a rage, grabbed a shovel I found leaning against the wall and began to smash in the cellar windows. The bright tinkling sound of glass shards lingered in the air for a moment after each blow had landed. When all five windows were gone, I tossed the shovel to the side and climbed through the empty window frames down into the cellar. Lucy was up. I didn't even look at her—went straight for the door with the little round window and opened it from the inside. With tiny footsteps, Lucy followed me up into the kitchen. Then she began to cry. I felt drained, as if I had no body, no muscles, no bones, but was made entirely of some soft, vaporlike substance. Lucy sat and wept while I grimly sliced bread for our supper.

The bus zooms up the hill into town. It's the last stop, and the old couple still hasn't moved. As I walk by them, I see that their heads are leaning against each other—they have fallen asleep.

I would have expected a house to feel empty after one of its inhabitants was gone, but in fact this house feels no different since Alois died. It's just that the pictures he hung aren't on the walls anymore. Some objects have disappeared, and the library's been cleaned out. Lucy has bought vases, bowls and baskets to put in the empty corners. But in my room nothing has changed at all. The floor is littered with the books I arrived with but have never read, postcards I've put stamps on but never mailed. I can't think of anyone to send them to.

My father writes me once a month. His letters come in thin envelopes and are never more than a page long. I really ought to open them more slowly, with a letter opener, but instead I tear through the envelopes as soon as they're in my hand. I read the letters while I'm going up the stairs and finish them before I get to my room. He always asks me to give his best to Lucy, but I never do it. I don't want her to look away and then not ask questions. Lucy has never asked questions.

From my bed I can see the sky, pure unchanging blue. Now and then a bird crosses through the pane of blue. I can hear the low booming of pile drivers from the neighboring town, where hotels and wide new streets are being built in expectation of the hundreds of thousands of pilgrims who will flock there in the year 2000. The town is a holy place, the site of some miracle. I envision the masses of people descending in a dark wave, all at once. If I live that long, I'll be twenty-four.

Looking at the bright sky outside gives me a headache, and in my search for painkillers I suddenly find myself in Lucy's room. The narrow bed by the window is unmade. Beyond it is a child's bed with old-fashioned dolls sitting up against the wall. I'm distracted from my quest and begin to examine the objects on Lucy's desk. Normally I would never do this—I know Lucy would be furious if she found me snooping around in her things—but somehow I feel entitled. Under a pad of paper I find a photograph: three people sitting under a tree with a lake in the background. Lucy, in the front with her eyes half-closed, seems to have glanced absently off to the side just as the shutter clicked. Alois has his arm around her, but it rests wooden and strange across her shoulder, and his gaze is directed at the third person in the picture, Paolo, Alois's musta-chioed art dealer from the city. Last summer, he invited Lucy and Alois to a party at his house, and they took me with them, perhaps only because Alois didn't want me alone in the house, unsupervised. The moment we got there, Lucy and Alois rushed off in opposite directions to say hello to different people. I knew no one and stood there alone in the entryway, completely useless.

I remember Paolo's house—it was made en-tirely of glass and light-colored granite, and the foyer shone smooth and bright in the setting sun. I caught a loose sentence floating through the air: "Wouldn't this foyer be great for roller-skating?" which annoyed me because anyone with eyes could have seen that the surface was slick as ice and you'd only destroy your knees if you tried it.

The guests were scattered in small groups across the manicured lawn. I was amazed to see how many people Lucy knew. Alois clearly knew them too but seemed not to value their company very highly. He had made himself comfortable in a shabby old leather armchair under a willow tree. He was squinting up at the sky and chain-smoking. I considered the possibility that he wasn't actually looking at the sky after all but watching the people. He might have some sort of x-ray vision that enabled him to be a voyeur, even while he appeared to gaze at the passing clouds. Just then he stretched out his legs and closed his eyes. The men Lucy was standing with opened their mouths and laughed in such a way that I could see their evenly spaced white teeth.

Lucy had given me a white dress to wear for the evening. I paraded around the house for hours wearing it and a pair of her high heels. I had come back to stand before the mirror again and again until I was sure that everything was just right, but there, at the party, I stood like a crumbling statue with a glass in my hand, hoping that no one would look at me at all. Motionlessly, I watched a column of ants run up and down the trunk of a tree—until suddenly someone tapped me on the shoulder. A gangly young man dressed entirely in light-colored linen planted himself before me.

"Only a weirdo could come up with this stuff," he said, referring to the numerous obscene putti that were standing on pedestals all across the lawn. "Paolo's my uncle. I should know," he added

"Oh. So, do you live here?" I asked.

"I just come for vacations, but if I had enough money, I'd go to a hotel instead."

"You don't like your uncle?"

"Like I said, he's a weirdo."

His small, blue eyes seemed to pierce right through me. Then he turned and pointed out the peacocks that were strutting about on the lawn as if they expected applause at any minute. I hadn't noticed them before.

"They act like runway models, as if they've spent weeks preening themselves just for this event," he said.

"Animals don't prepare themselves for anything," I said.

He looked back over at the peacocks.

After a while he said, "I write poetry, when I can find the time." The expectant look on his face made me nervous. I had no idea how to respond to such an announcement, so I looked noncommittally off into the willow trees. Then, without really thinking it over, I said willows were sad trees and that their branches bent to the earth under the weight of the world's tears. The words jammed up in my mouth before I had finished speaking and came out awkwardly.

He looked ponderously into his glass and spoke in a voice as thin as rain. "I think we're similar, you and me. I'm going to put that beautiful idea down for you, in verse." Then he asked me if I wanted to go to a techno party with him the following Saturday, crossing his fingers and kissing them as he spoke. "I swear it's going to be a megacool party."

Before I could respond to the invitation, Lucy came up to us. She looked especially beautiful that night because she was excited. It was the first time she'd left the house in weeks. She reached out her hand to him.

"I'm related to Paolo," he said, this time as if it were something to be glad about. "You must be Jo's sister?"

"No, her mother," she laughed, clapping him on the shoulder and then moving off to talk to a group of people a few yards away. They were laughing boisterously. I didn't move, but suddenly I felt his breath against the side of my throat.

"How old are you, actually?" he asked in a penetrating voice.

"Fifteen." I was a full three years older than that, but I saw no point in telling him the truth.

I watched his back as he sauntered across the grass, wide and tall in his linen jacket, and disappeared into the house. In the meantime Alois had fallen asleep in his armchair. I could have gone over to him, shaken him awake and said, Come on, let's go. You can't stand this party either, can you? Let's drive back to the house, right now. But instead I stood silently in front of him and stared at the way his mouth hung open, his head tilted off to one side. His hands were clasped over his belly, and an empty pack of Gauloises lay crumpled on the grass beside his chair. Why, I wondered, did Alois smoke

Gauloises? There were thousands of brands of cigarettes in the world, but Alois had chosen Gauloises.
God only knew why. I certainly didn't plan to ask
him, but I resolved to stand there, contemplating
meaningless questions, until he awoke.

I T ' S S T I L L light out, and I hope
that Lucy will return before nightfall. I put the
snapshot back where I found it, under the pad. It
was taken three years ago, at a time when I didn't
have any idea I'd be coming here. That didn't happen until after I graduated. When I held my di-
ploma in my hands, I began to wonder whether I
wanted to go straight to university or if maybe I
shouldn't take a little time off to travel. I realized
there was no way I was going right back to school,
and I decided to go and visit my mother, whom I
hadn't seen in twelve years. I got myself a hotel
room in the city near the town where she lived and
called her from a pay phone. I had imagined the
conversation many times, but as I stood there and
raised the receiver to my ear, I watched it shake
violently in my grasp. I had to wait some time for
that to subside.

The moment I heard her voice, the long-
prepared sentences tumbled from my mouth in an
indecipherable tangle. The word *mother* and the

voice on the other end of the line were two separate things, both of them enormous, towering over me. I flinched at the silence on the line as if it were a blow. The receiver was dead in my hand. It seemed for a moment that everything inside the phone booth had come to a standstill. Traffic and people went by outside, but I was locked in a bubble of time.

"Hello? Who's there?" asked my mother impatiently.

I heard my voice speak my name. I told her I wanted to visit her. It seemed shameless somehow, as if I had asked a complete stranger to do me a great favor. I was afraid I would hear the dial tone again, but then there came a laugh, laughter that went on and on and did not want to stop.

"My daughter is calling me up to ask if she can come visit me?"

It sounded like she found the request absurdly ponderous and complicated, so I said I didn't think I could just show up all of a sudden after twelve years. She was laughing again, about the twelve years, asking if it could really have been so long. At last she told me that her house was always open to me. I went back to the hotel and packed up my belongings.

●

FOR HOURS I have been fighting sleep. I flip to the TV show that has the most screaming and gunfire, hoping the noise will keep me awake. I don't want to be asleep when Lucy gets home. I am overwhelmed with the feeling that something is missing. I have no idea how many cop shows I've watched. Women are continuously strangled in their beds, men shot in underground garages.

Then I hear the footsteps approaching quickly, heels ringing against the asphalt of the alleyway. Lucy. I turn down the volume on the TV and listen as she pauses at the front door to search for her keys. She enters and climbs the stairs. I think I hear her yawning, and then she opens the door to her room and closes it quietly behind her as if she didn't want to wake anyone up. But she must have seen the light in my window. Surely she'll come out in a moment, I think, as I get up and go to the kitchen.

I start to wipe off the table, just to do something while I wait for her to emerge from her room. The longer I wait, the stranger my hand looks as it travels back and forth across the table. It takes some time for me to realize that she won't be coming out. She won't be telling me anything, because she's already fast asleep, dreaming.

•

THE BARKING dog comes nearer and nearer, but my feet are rooted to the ground. My face drips with sweat. I wrench my head around to look the dog in the face. Saliva glints on its pink gums and sharp teeth, which grow ever larger as the dog comes nearer. I want to call him off, but turning to look at him has only egged him on. He crouches before me, ready to pounce. I am crazed with fear and I reach out to grab his muzzle, taking the upper jaw in one hand, the lower in the other. With all my might I tear his snout in two. It makes a cracking noise, like a loaf of stale bread breaking. The sound stays with me as I slide slowly, smoothly, from my dream and find myself back in bed. I lie there, motionless, an empty vessel that fills itself over and over with the recollection of where I am. The sheet is crumpled into a ball at the foot of the bed. I blink at the ceiling in that exhausted, euphoric state that always comes over me when I've managed to save myself from some terrible fate in a dream. I notice that there really is a dog barking outside my window, harmlessly, inconsequentially barking, and I smile.

In the past few days I have hardly been able to eat at all, and my stomach is caved in, creating a hollow between my jutting hipbones. A warm wind filters through the half-open window. I close my eyes, hoping to fall into a peaceful, dreamless slumber, but the pile drivers have started up in the neighboring town, ripping through the earth, chasing me from bed.

On the stairs I catch a whiff of Lucy's lemony bath oil. I peek through the open bathroom door and see Lucy sitting in the tub with her hair piled up, surrounded by a cloud of vapor. She silently points her finger at the chair where her clothes are draped, indicating that I should sit down.

"Will you be around tonight?" I ask.

"Sorry, Jo. I have plans."

She pushes the washcloth up and down along the length of her bent leg. There's something awkward and compulsive about it, and I redirect my gaze to the shampoo bottle at the edge of the tub.

"Listen, Jo." Her voice is forceful. "I don't plan to spend the next thirty summers of my life playing the widow. I told you before, I'm done with that business."

She tries to catch my eye, but I'm still staring at the shampoo. *Robert's*, it says.

When she speaks, it sounds like she's telling a story that doesn't particularly matter to her one way or the other. "You came here because you wanted to see me. Nobody could have predicted that Alois would have that accident. I had a bit of a breakdown, as you know, and you tried to help me. But, Jo, I don't need your help. Okay? Do you understand that?"

Lucy wrings the water vigorously from the cloth, using both hands.

"So what was I supposed to do, leave you lying there?"

I shout the words, but Lucy isn't listening anymore. She pulls the shower curtain closed with a quick jerk and turns on the water.

I leave the house without eating breakfast. A paved road leads from the village to the adjacent forest. I pass by a café that never seems to be open and a parking lot that's larger than the mini-golf course it serves. I've never seen a single person playing. You can see the cement through the peeling paint of the putting greens. A narrow path leads from the parking lot into the woods. Butterflies flit like colorful puffs of smoke from the bushes. Insects fly into my face and settle on my bare arms, and I swat them away with my hand. The vegetation grows wildly in every direction, threatening either to overgrow the path or strangle itself. Trees soar from the earth and project a canopy of leaves across the heavens.

The air is so thick with the scent of flowers that I grow faintly nauseated as I climb a steep incline to the edge of a small cliff. From there I look out at a river that flows over a broad expanse of rock and into a bathtub-sized pool that has been gouged from the rock. The river flows through a notch in the pool and drops maybe twenty-five feet onto the wider riverbed below. I sit on the rock, take off my shoes and dangle my feet in the pool. With my ten toes I scatter the countless tadpoles— tiny black flecks that cling to the side of the basin. I lean forward and watch the water pour over the edge in a fat stream, a polished rod of crystal that shatters with a roar into a cloud of white slivers at the bottom. I lie back on the warm stone. I should just stay here, I think, until I become a part of this stone. At first, perhaps, noisy people would come to take a dip in the pool, but eventually the path would seal itself off and it would be quiet here. Moss would grow over me, the tadpoles would be gone, and even the water would subside.

A butterfly tickles my elbow, creeps across my outstretched arm, onto my hand, my fingertips, and steps out onto the water. I sit up to watch as it glides across the surface and is carried away. The water sucks at its wings and the current propels it toward the downspout until it falls into the cascade. And then I realize that there are dozens of butterflies stepping off the stone into the pool. Some drop themselves into the water from the air. I pull a long blade of grass from a crack between two rocks and intercept one of them. It holds on tightly, and I pull it from the water. I rescue more and more of them in this way, until the rock is crowded with butterflies drying their crumpled wings. After a short time, they fold up their wings and fly in a straight line, one after the other, back into the fatal water.

Lucy once brought me to this place. "I'm going to take you to the most peaceful place I know," she said. The morning was already warm when we arrived, and we stretched out on the stone in our bathing suits. The stone lay idle, naked in the sun. There were no shadows. I was so pleased to be spending the day with her, but the heat quickly drained me of energy. As I was depleted, Lucy grew livelier. She seemed to know everything about the plants that were growing all around us, and I grew sleepier and sleepier as I listened to their strange names as if from a great distance. Just as I was about to melt away entirely under the hard sun, I struggled to my feet and plunged into the pool of icy springwater. It roused me, and I splashed exuberantly, churning the water with my arms and legs.

The spray glittered in the air, thousands of rainbow-colored droplets fracturing the light, and I wanted to call out to Lucy to join me in the water. But then I turned and saw the look on her face. She was eyeing me as if I were her enemy. I stopped splashing and climbed quickly from the water. When I was back on the rock, the cool, refreshing drops of water dried on my skin and the heat began to envelop me once again.

"It's deadly hot," I panted a short while later and sat up with my head buzzing. I was going to suggest that we find a spot in the shade somewhere, but, when I looked over to where she was sitting, I let out a scream instead. There, in the shimmering heat, I saw nothing but a dark silhouette, a hole in the light.

That night my heart raged in my breast like a penned beast. I thrashed in my sheets, drenching them. Sweat poured from my body as if a terrible sun burned inside it.

Not a single butterfly remains behind. They all go over the falls. The street back to town is bright under the midday sun; the air above the asphalt wavers with heat. I decide I want to tell the story of the butterflies to Lucy and set off up the road toward the house, going faster and faster until finally I'm running so as not to miss her. The spittle in my mouth dries up and blood pounds in my temples as I turn off by the monastery onto our lane. Giuseppe, our neighbor, is sitting on a stool in front of his house and greets me sullenly. I slow down a moment, thinking to ask him if he's seen her, but then press on, preferring to find her for myself. I run inside, calling out her name as soon as I'm on the stairs. I look in her bedroom, the kitchen, the bathroom, then her room a second time. She's gone. Her bathrobe lies on the floor beside the bed. The closet door stands open. I sit down on the bed and take note of these details as if they were left deliberately, clues to her hurried departure.

I realize as I look around me that she's moved

the bed away from its former place by the window. The day I arrived, when she gave me the tour of the house, Lucy told me that the first thing she did in the morning was to look out her bedroom window at the view of the old monastery wall and, behind it, the row of poplars that grows in the cemetery. Now that Alois's grave lies beneath them, the poplars are living tombstones. Lucy can't stand memories—they weigh her down—and so she's moved the bed just a few inches over to avoid the view. As if you could just erase the life of a human being by destroying his property and moving your bed so you don't have to look at the trees that stand by his grave. She won't put the bed back where it was until those trees have been chopped down and the view of the hills and sky is clear, an uninterrupted expanse that reminds her of nothing.

The wide-open closet door and the carelessly dropped robe are decoys, intended to divert attention from the more important signs of Lucy's attempt to erase her memory.

After she led me through her room the day I arrived, we went to the kitchen and she stooped down to show me the supplies that were kept on the bottom shelf: jars and jars of preserves, coated with dust from long standing. She told me she'd stopped putting things up a couple of years before, since she and Alois could never eat it all. We heard footsteps approaching the kitchen and she stood up straight, unaware she was doing it, as if she were frightened or about to be surprised in some illicit activity. She seemed to feel threatened, to be in some danger. She held up a jar of preserved pears, awkwardly, between her thumb and index finger, as if she were pointing to the jar. Alois stared fixedly at the jar as he moved through the kitchen, never looking at Lucy, only at the pears. When he was in front of us, he shifted his gaze to me. It was angry and derisive, oddly in contrast to the expression on his lips, which, thanks to the deep creases at the corners of his mouth, always seemed to be smiling. He extended his hand to me reluctantly, making no secret of the fact that he would have preferred I hadn't come.

For dinner we sat at the round table in the dining room. A small television set was playing in the background with the sound turned down. You could see a group of politicians standing behind a table and waving their arms in agitation. Lucy was explaining to me why she never went to town. There were nothing but old men sitting around in the bar playing cards and staring at every stranger who passed through. It was quite clear, she said, that the people in this town were cut off from everything that happened in the real world.

With the exception of one brief, heated exchange with Lucy, Alois remained silent throughout the meal. I understood only that some newspaper article had annoyed him. He stared tensely at his plate or looked over Lucy's head at the television screen. They spoke in a strange language composed of words I didn't understand, and the strange grunts and noises that couples sometimes develop over time, when they are always alone with each other and cut off from the outside world. As they spoke, I looked at the two paintings hanging side by side on the far wall. In brilliant colors that began to hurt my eyes the longer I looked at them, each painting depicted a tree that had been struck by lightning. In the lower right corner, barely legible, was Alois's signature. Aside from the table where we sat and an enormous sofa, the room was empty. In a wall niche that might have been designed to hold a statue of the Virgin Mary, there stood a large vase and a pair of tiny blue ballet shoes. Lucy must have noticed me looking at them, because she explained she'd bought them for me in town during the first few weeks after she moved here, but then she had forgotten to mail them. They'd be a bit small now, she said, looking unkindly at my rather too large feet.

M Y   R O O M was in the top part of the house, and, like all the others, it was marked by a kind of stingy bareness, as if no one was supposed to be able to tell that anyone lived there. I didn't notice the painting on the wall until I lay down on the bed that first night: another lightning-blasted tree, like the ones downstairs. I tried to roll over and close my eyes, but it was impossible. The painting demanded that I look at it. The tree was split down the middle, and light-colored wood spewed out from the center. It was a realistic depiction, bordered with a pattern of acanthus tendrils and geometric ornaments. The paint was laid on with a palette knife, so thickly in places that it protruded from the canvas. The colors were shrill, piercing the air, setting it aquiver like a high-pitched tone beyond the range of human hearing. The atmosphere of the room was highly charged, and I tossed and turned and thrashed. It was impossible to fall asleep with that painting on the wall. It demanded that I look at it. Even more unbearable than the loud colors was the ornamental frieze around the shattered tree, a cynical mockery of a natural disaster. I jumped out of bed and began to take the painting off the wall, but just then there came a knock on the door. Lucy asked if she could come in. I hastily returned the painting to its hook and climbed back under the covers.

Lucy came in and sat on the edge of my bed. Instinctively, I moved away, half to make room for her, half because it was so strange to be near her, but I regretted doing it immediately, because she rose up again in response and stood at the window with her back to me. She said that we would not discuss the past. She did not feel obligated to make amends to me, and if that's what I wanted, she couldn't help me. I reassured her that I'd had nothing of the sort in mind. I would have felt better if I could have stood beside her, but I was immobilized within my cocoon of pajamas and bedclothes.

Even after she left and I took the painting down again, I didn't sleep. I couldn't stop thinking about the shoes she had forgotten to send to me. I imagined how I would have strolled about in my father's apartment, wearing them. I would have used them as houses, or boats, for Nico and Florian to sit in as they watched over me at night from their places beside my bed. Finally, I got out of bed feeling as if I'd just lost a long, arduous battle, and went to the window. Beneath me lay the garden, and if I leaned out far enough I could see the kitchen window. It was still brightly lit, and I could see Lucy and Alois's shadows. They were sitting at the table talking. I leaned out the window as far as I possibly could, but I wasn't able to make out a single word from the muffled hum of their voices.

IN THE next town, the pile drivers are back at work. The sound wears me down as much as the idea that somewhere right nearby the earth is being ripped up, reshaped and feverishly built upon. There was a time when none of this would have bothered me at all. The noise would not have been important enough for me even to notice it. I would have walled it off behind the words of some book. I've been able to escape reality by reading ever since I can remember. A wall of words encircled and protected me as long as I read, and so I did nothing else. Even when I wasn't reading, I could always conjure up the characters from the stories I'd read and have conversations with them in my head. I must have had thousands of such conversations as I sat, silent and well behaved, at my school desk.

DURING VACATIONS from school, I used to sort letters at the post office. When I read the names on envelopes that had been hand-addressed, characters sprang up in my head and began to speak while I sat there, unobserved, and listened to them. It seemed to me that I had found a hidden access into the lives of strangers. They didn't know me, but because I'd held their names, their handwriting, between my fingers, they occupied a space within me, a place where they were free to dwell and to proliferate. It was as if I were the keeper of their secret lives.

At the end of every month I met with Father, and he gave me my allowance. I'd been living on my own in a room in the city since I turned sixteen. It was empty there, like the room in this house, but, there I never felt lost. When I read, I became a ship on a voyage. From time to time, I was overtaken by fits of exhaustion so great that I could no longer even lift a book. When that happened, I called Father. He came for me in his Buick and we drove away together. I would look past his hands, holding the wheel, at the houses of the city and, later, at the fir trees and the guardrail flashing past. The headlights bored through the darkness to illuminate the surface of the roadway. The car hummed along, and we would smoke cigarettes until the interior of the car was thick with smoke, as if we had been caught in the fog. I made believe that we were in flight together. It made me happy to think of fleeing with my father. The lights of the car in front of us left a red trail on the asphalt, which our car swallowed up as we overtook it. Sometimes Father would speak, very quietly, as if to himself.

SINCE I'VE been here I haven't read a single line. Even now, I can't. I lie here as if I'd been snapped off at the vine, staring at the whitewashed wall before me. Then it occurs to me that perhaps Lucy keeps a journal. I go to her closet like a thief to look for it. I open every drawer and rummage around in her underwear. As I look, the book that I had first imagined as thick and heavy dwindles to a thin notebook. Somewhere in here there must be at least this notebook. When I stand on a chair to search the top shelf, I nearly send a vase crashing down to the floor. I put everything back, just as it was, cursing my failure.

Back in my room, I pick out one of my books and light a cigarette. Lying on the bed, my head propped up by a pillow, I crack the spine. The taste of the cigarette smoke is sharp. Until I grow accustomed to it, it makes the words dance up and down on the page. They swim before my eyes. I read the first line over and over without advancing to the second. Once, I went through words like open doors. Now I stand before them and nothing happens. It's simply too great a strain to follow this train of words that leads nowhere except to a period and then another sentence—more words. I am locked out.

I close the book with resignation and watch the smoke from my cigarette take on the shapes of animals. The little creatures climb from my lips to the ceiling, which is a field for them to play in, though most never make it that far. They erase themselves before they get there. I try to blow them out in big enough puffs that they will survive the trip. Hunger, a hollow nagging pain, interrupts my game, but I'm not in the mood to go downstairs and sit by myself in the dining room.

THOUGH IT is early morning, the air in the garden is already warm. Lucy reads a newspaper in the shadow of the palm tree. Her hair is pulled back tight, and her face is smeared with a beauty mask that smells like cucumbers. When I sit down beside her she lets the paper fall to the ground. She has avoided applying the mask in the area around her eyes, so that her two blue irises gaze out at me from flesh-colored circles.

"I've invited a friend over tonight," she says. "Vito. You'll like him."

Then she picks her paper back up.

"I'd like to know what you do here all day, the whole time when I'm away." She makes it sound like an offhand question, but the curiosity in her voice is unmistakable.

"I read. I have a huge pile of books in my room. Last night I read till late at night." Even as I'm saying it, I can tell it sounds like I'm on the defensive.

I go inside to get breakfast, and when I return with the tray of bread, cheese and honey, I hear the birds screeching in Giuseppe's cellar. Up until his wife died of a stroke a short time ago, you could see the old couple's shadows moving behind the windows in the evening and hear him berating her. Now there's just the noise of the birds screeching when he goes down to the cellar to slaughter one for the table. Lucy thinks he's crazy. I put the platter down on the table. Lucy has her chin propped up on her hand and looks nervously over at the monastery.

"Listen, Jo. I haven't told Vito anything about you. I mean, he has no idea that I have a daughter. And I thought that we could maybe tell him a sort of half-truth—that you're my younger sister."

"Oh, sure. No problem," I say quickly, flatly, as if I expected this and had been practicing for the moment for years. She runs her hand through her hair as if she feels young and energetic. Clearly, she's relieved. Lucy babbles in a light, unconcerned tone, but I hardly hear what she says. My body is rigid except for an occasional nod, and my eyes are fixed on the now dried-up cucumber mask that has slowly begun to flake and crumble off of her face. Larger and larger pieces detach themselves from her skin and drop into her lap. Then she raises her hands to her face as if she wanted to hold it together, to keep it from falling apart entirely. She excuses herself and hurries off to the bath, where she spends almost the entire day.

On the sofa in the dining room I hold a book

propped open on my knees. The words on the page are useless to me now, and I think of Alois, lying dead beneath the poplars, growing ever more so. Lucy finally reemerges from the bathroom in a long, swingy black skirt that bells out at the bottom and a bright blue blouse. As she comes into the dining room and sits down, I catch a whiff of her clean-smelling perfume. Out of the corner of my eye I can see her profile. Her freshly washed hair is tucked virginally behind her ears. A dark feeling rises up in me. I am suddenly bursting to ask her if it's really true that she left my father and went away in an airplane—or if everything might not have happened completely differently, if she's certain that I actually came out of her body. Because at this moment it seems completely improbable to me. She looks over at me, and I quickly turn the page.

"What would you do, Jo, if this house suddenly belonged to you?" She rises from the table and comes toward me.

"Rent it out to some family," I say without even considering it. The way she's standing, her skirt seems to shelter me like the wing of a great black bird. For just a moment, it seems this might last. Me sitting here, her standing before me like a great rock, a boulder. I feel her eyes burning into my head but am afraid to meet them, to see them cold and hard above the wing of her skirt.

•

L U C Y ' S   I N   the kitchen making dinner for Vito. I wait in the garden, frozen in place,
hoping that she'll ask me to come in and help her
cook. I wait to hear her voice, but she doesn't call.
I listen to her footsteps going back and forth. I hear
the clattering pans. With my eyes still open, I slip
into a waking dream in which I imagine myself
much younger. My mother stands in the kitchen
preparing our supper while I do my homework at
the table. The noises Lucy actually makes provide
the sound track for the daydream. They are a tape
that bores into my head through my ears as it plays.
Somewhere within me, her every sound is recorded
and preserved so that, when this is over, I'll be able
to call her up again, remember her face, talk to her,
even though she's not really there. The sharp ring
of the doorbell penetrates through the house to
where I sit in the garden, and I hear Lucy put something down on the stove with a bang and hurry
downstairs. As she takes him though the house, the
metal taps on his shoes click against the floor. Vito's
laugh echoes through Alois's emptied-out library.
In the hall, Lucy and Vito stand motionlessly at the
window and peer out at the garden. They're looking
in my direction but they don't see me, even when I
wave. I recognize the outline of his head, which is

too large for his narrow shoulders. His hair is shiny
and combed back smooth against his scalp. Alois
once stood at the window that way. I bumped into
him on the way back to my room from the kitchen.
He was wearing his work clothes and holding a
paintbrush full of wet paint. He set it down on the
sill.

"Do you think a house can just suddenly collapse upon itself, like a dying person?" he asked
me. "One crisis, and that's it—the beginning of the
end." He spoke without looking at me. Alois had
never asked me anything before, so I assumed he
must have thought it was Lucy standing there.

"Maybe so," I said, uncertainly, looking at the
paintbrush as it dripped yellow on the floor.

LUCY OPENS the garden door for
Vito. He notices me, and Lucy winks conspiratorially from behind the rosebush when he calls out:
"Ah, you must be the little sister!" He covers the
distance from the house to my lounge chair with his
hand extended toward me. He overwhelms me with
questions, presses my hand lightly in his and looks
at me intently. His eyes are encircled by countless
tiny wrinkles. Lucy has set the table in the garden
and carries the food out in great bowls. Vito wants
to know what I do for a living and, unprepared for

such questions, I respond that I work at the post office sorting mail. His eyes grow smaller and seem almost about to disappear into the nest of wrinkles until Lucy laughs and adds that the post office job is only temporary and I will be going to university next year.

"Oh, of course," Vito laughs, and we clink our glasses.

The wine is too warm. The heat hangs heavy in the air this evening, mounting and mounting with no relief in sight. My skin and everything I touch are coated with a thin, sticky film. The red heads of the geraniums on the monastery's parapet wall hang limply, although they were watered only a short time ago. Vito says he's in the hotel business and incredibly busy right now. He's building a chain of hotels for the year 2000, when a hundred thousand pilgrims are expected. Some of the hotels are already booked solid, even though they aren't built yet. "We've got to be prepared for this influx of people," he says, over and over, and breathes through his nose like a snorting hippopotamus. Lucy and Vito talk all through dinner, so much, so fast, that I am buried in the avalanche of words and sit there, deaf and dumb, without even trying to follow their conversation. When Vito talks, I can see his front teeth, a row of small white stumps. He interrupts Lucy constantly but it doesn't seem to bother her. She just nods enthusiastically at what-

ever he says. She seems to be taken in by his voice
and the clear, bright sound of his lighter flicking at
regular intervals. Glistening droplets of sweat bead
on Vito's brow and the tip of his nose. At one point,
he half stands and drags his chair closer to Lucy, so
that he's sitting directly between me and the monastery poplars. It looks as though they're growing
from the top of his head. I get up hastily, clear the
table and do my best to vanish.

From the kitchen I can still make out their
voices growing ever louder until they wrap around
one another and weave themselves into a cocoon of
words. Lucy's tittering in the midst of Vito's tossed-
out laughter seems to contain not a shred of pleasure, no joy, just a false self-satisfaction.

T H E   A I R lies over the town like a dark,
rustling sheet of silk. The square with the church
and the fountain in the middle is a vessel that collects the townspeople and brings them together. It
buzzes with children shouting, men talking, women
laughing. In front of the bar, old men sit wearing
slippers and slouching over their cards. The light
from the bar shines out onto the square. Only the
unadorned church across the way is completely
dark.

Walking along the little alleyway, I come to the

old gate in the city wall. From here on out, there is only the barking of dogs—no sign of the activity taking place on the square. With the wall at my back, I look down at the city on the plain below. The bright streets grope their way outward to the surrounding forest, curving like an insect's antennae. Beyond, the spine of the mountains juts up and stretches across the horizon. A few days after my arrival here, Lucy and I went up there, to the mountains. We set out from the house early in the morning, planning to explore the area. Lucy showed me countless little villages, all of which seemed to be built of light-colored stone and inhabited exclusively by old men and cats. At last, when we were exhausted by the heat and the sight of so many fields of tobacco and sunflowers, we headed up the mountain. We drove through forests and thickets for half an hour with the branches of young trees scratching at the windows. At the top, we walked across the sparse, sun-bleached grass. From there, the villages we'd just passed through looked like uneven blotches on the landscape. There was nothing where we stood, not a single tree, just a great dizzying open space. I could feel my heart pounding against the inside of my sweater. I would have liked to sink to the ground and never budge again, but there was Lucy, tossing her head in the wind and laughing, prattling on about the view as proudly as if she'd made it herself.

"It would be pretty creepy up here alone at night, don't you think?" I asked her. She looked over at me as if I'd said something completely irrelevant, and suddenly the ground seemed to buck under my feet as if I were riding on the back of an unbroken beast. The sky threatened to open wide, and I felt the hardness of the earth beneath me. I tried to concentrate on the mole under the left corner of Lucy's mouth, but her face broke up into pieces as she leaned over me, peering into my eyes.

When I came to I was lying in the back of the car, curled up under a blanket, the motor purring under my body. The smell of fresh bread had woken me up. I looked at the back of Lucy's head sticking up motionlessly from behind the beige headrest, her hands gripping the wheel. Rain pounded the roof of the car and ran streaming across the windows. I felt oddly content, satisfied. I smiled to myself.

The church bells are tolling one o'clock. Vito will surely sleep over at the house tonight. I make my way slowly back to the town square. The bar is still open—only the women and children have gone home. I stride through the door with its colored plastic strips and sit at the bar. In the next room three men are playing pool. The clicking of the balls is accompanied by frequent yelling and cursing. Sitting next to me is a heavy man in a checked shirt that's come untucked from his pants. He takes one pistachio after another from a little bag, cracks the shells with his teeth and spits them out onto the surface of the bar. The bartender watches me suspiciously from the corner of his eye for a while before asking what I'd like to drink. I order a glass of port and take it to an empty table where I can catch the action at the pool table. Two of the players move in the same lumbering manner. They seem to be brothers. Their mouths hang open and their eyelids droop as if they are both on the verge of dozing off. The third, a pale, sickly-looking, hollow-cheeked youth, circles the table continuously and bangs his pool cue on the floor. I can tell they've noticed me because they keep looking over in my direction and talking so I can hear. The young one looks me straight in the face without smiling. When he leans over the felt, his hair falls in front of his eyes. I don't know the first thing about pool, but I watch them like I'm following every move. Suddenly, in the middle of a game, the brothers both put their cues in the rack and walk over to the bar. The young one protests, pounding his stick more vigorously now, but the brothers have already ordered drinks and insinuated themselves into a conversation between the bartender and the pistachio eater.

"Yeah, it's always like this. Whenever they realize I'm winning, they quit," he yells, loudly enough for the room at large to hear him, though he's looking at, talking to, me. Then he picks up a bottle of port and brings it over to my table. He asks me if I'm related to the foreigner. I realize he must mean Lucy, so I say yes, I'm her sister. The idea that she might actually just be my sister is somehow such a relief that I resolve always to introduce her that way in the future.

"Luciano," the youth says and reaches out to shake my hand. The brothers laugh and turn around to stare at us repeatedly. Luciano tells me he's heard my sister's husband was killed in the car crash. He says he witnessed it, he was standing right there, at the bottom of the hill. I nod silently. When we take the bus, Lucy always looks away from the window before we pass the spot where it happened. We have crossed over that place in the road dozens of times by now, always in silence. There is still a patch of blackened earth where the car burned. No part of Alois's body was actually recovered, not even any of the ashes, which were scattered by the high winds that day. Rolled and exploded, the police report said. It didn't occur to anyone that he might have done it on purpose. Lucy spent so long talking to Dr. Alberti about the horrible, tragic accident that even she now believes that's what happened. In fact though, Alois had been thinking about how to kill himself for a long time. In the cellar room, while he mixed his paints; during meals; in the mornings when he awoke with Lucy curled up like a fetus beside him. And that day, when he stood despondent at the window and asked me if a house could collapse as suddenly as a person at the end of life. He already knew it then. Two days later I was home watching television when the phone rang. "Hello, this is City Hospital. Are Lucy and Alois Hagenbach your parents?" The voice was female. I could barely comprehend her words. On the screen, two enemy gangs were rumbling on the grounds of an abandoned factory. "Yes," I said. "I mean no. I mean, Lucy is my mother."

"Mr. Hagenbach has had a serious car accident. Your mother is here too," said the voice. On the bus ride to the hospital I peered out the window at the curb as if through a magnifying glass. Grass grew through cracks in the asphalt. I counted the empty cigarette packs and other pieces of garbage that had been thrown from car windows. Near town, I saw the body of a cat, swollen in the heat, that had been scooped up and pushed to the edge of the road. There was no doubt in my mind that Alois had intentionally caused the accident. I remember the dark red entranceway of the hospital down to the last detail, the café full of old tittering biddies in long flowered nightgowns squashing bits of cake in the tines of their forks before putting them into their mouths. I stared at the receptionist's name tag while she looked up Lucy's room number in the computer. FRAU JASINOVIC. "Room 237," she said in a voice that would have been perfect for reading to children.

"You read to your children, don't you? From the *Thousand and One Nights?*" I think I actually asked her that, and as I remember it, she leaned toward me, so close that I could feel her warm breath on my face. It made me think of a basket of freshly washed laundry. "You don't have to worry. Your mother is already doing much better. Room 237." I ran through the hospital's endless corridors, past red upholstered chairs in waiting areas and shiny-leafed rubber plants and sleepwalking nurses pushing stretchers on which I could see only low arching forms concealed under brown woolen blankets, and the whole time I thought of Signora Jasinovic. I wanted her always to be there and to read from the *Thousand and One Nights*. I wandered lost in this labyrinth for some time before I came to room 237, but then, when I got there, I didn't go in right away. There was no hurry any more. Alois— the hiding place in which Lucy had concealed herself from me, the longtime protector of Lucy's secrets, the hungry predator that devoured the ground on which I sought to walk—was gone. I thought that a smooth white door was about to swing open and Lucy's life would henceforth transpire before my eyes. The time had come at last for me to become a part of Lucy's life.

•

LUCIANO LEADS me from the bar with his hand on my elbow. The brothers are keeping pace with us on the other side of the street, where the church is, and Luciano tells them to beat it. They disappear behind the church, howling with laughter. The bartender closes the door and turns out the light, so that now the only light in the square comes from within the fountain. Luciano keeps hold of my elbow until we're sitting down on the steps by the fountain. I can't remember anything he said to me in the bar, just that he got up frequently to bring more port. There are figures carved into the stone of the fountain and they smile out at us stoically. I ask Luciano if he knows who they represent.

"I don't know, some saints, I guess," he says and tugs at my sleeve. "Let's get out of here."

His room is on the top floor of an apartment house and it's brutally hot. Only a whisper of fresh air makes it through the open skylight. Next to the mattress in the corner are a boom box and a small chest. On top of the chest, behind a candle and a plastic rose, stands a gold-framed newspaper clipping about Kurt Cobain. An altar. Newspapers and dirty clothes are strewn about. He tells me he's heading off to the city in a week to find a job and start a band. He's going to be the singer. He pushes me into an armchair in the middle of the room, gets some beer from the kitchen and lies down on the mattress. There's a yellowish fluorescent light in the room that gives Luciano's face an even more sickly cast and brings out the dark circles under his eyes. We discover that we have the same birthday, and that starts us laughing hysterically, uncontrollably. His hand shakes when he's laughing, and he spills beer in the bed, which gets us laughing even harder.

"So, uh, do you think I look sick?" he asks me all of the sudden.

"Well, yeah, I guess you do, if I look closely."

"Okay, cool. A singer should look as sick as possible." He brushes a few strands of hair away from his face and turns on the CD player. The voice of Kurt Cobain rattles through the room. Luciano tells me he's just lost his job as a cook because the restaurant he worked at was torn down to make room for one of the new hotels. He laughs angrily and takes another slug of beer.

"Yeah, I'm out of here next week anyway."

"Those two guys you were playing pool with —are they your friends?" I ask him.

"The Palmisano brothers, my friends?" He laughs. "Those two are the village idiots. Like, kids in town tell Palmisano brothers jokes, you know? They're not quite right upstairs." He taps the side of his head. They've got this idea they both want to play the role of Jesus at the Easter festival, but the organizers won't let them." He pulls a photo out of a drawer and shows it to me. "Look at this—I did it one year."

The picture shows a crowd of people parading across the village square. Out in front is Luciano, dressed as Jesus and tied to a great cross that is being borne aloft by four men. Every year in this town, they celebrate Easter by tying one of the village youths to the cross and marching him through the streets.

Luciano starts to sing into his beer bottle as if it were a microphone. His voice is hoarse and totally off key, and I laugh at him at the top of my voice from my armchair, but that doesn't stop him from raising his voice and singing on even louder. I get up to find something to drink in the kitchen. Dirty dishes are stacked shoulder high in the sink. There's one pan with food still in it, so thick with mold that the contents are unrecognizable. The screen of the vent over the stove is crusted with yellow. Luciano must have done a lot of cooking here in the past, but now it's filthy. It's clear he's moving on. In amongst the empty packages and crumbs I spot a crumpled-up business card with his name on it and the address of the restaurant.

As I search for a clean glass, I come upon an azalea plant perched in between two piles of dishes. The earth is dry and the leaves have all fallen off. I put it under running water until the dirt is moist through. When I go back into the other room, I see that Luciano has gotten into bed. He's under the covers with his eyes closed, and his clothes lie in a heap beside the mattress. He's asleep. A bit of beer dribbles onto the carpet from the mouth of the overturned bottle, which rests in the curl of Luciano's pale hand, a sliver of waning moon. The stairs creak, and I feel like a criminal as I quietly make my exit on tiptoe. It's a horrible thing to descend a stairwell at night, passing doors behind which strangers are sleeping. I imagine enormous beds just on the other side of the walls, people snuggled tightly together, their sleeping bodies forming warm, breathing hills—and when my noise awakens them, the ground begins to quake. I think I can hear someone cursing in one of the apartments.

Finally, I'm outside again, and my footsteps echo loudly through the sleeping town. It's just the sound of my own feet, but it bothers me, so I slip off my shoes. The air is pleasantly cool, but the pavement radiates heat from the day into the soles of my feet. I imagine that the earth I tread on is the top layer of skin of a living creature, perhaps some sort of sea lion. Somehow this idea makes me feel at peace, and I take the detour along the city wall and look out onto the plain once more. The mountains are gone, subsumed into the black wall of night. Even the city in between has been largely erased. Just a few lights twinkle sporadically in the distance, as if they were agitated by their dreams.

S L E E P   I S dark. Rays of sunshine penetrate the slats of the Venetian blinds. I wake up sticky and damp, searching for a cool spot on the bed, out of the sun, so I can doze a while longer. I lie there, torn, broiling in the sun but unable to get up. My bones are like jelly. At last I admit it's no use. Sleep has abandoned me. Downstairs in the kitchen the dishes are stacked neatly in the cabinets. The old gas oven and the cupboard sparkle. On the kitchen table there is a note.

Spending the weekend at Vito's.
—Lucy

I put the kettle on the stove and sit at the table. A faint scream echoes in my head, followed by a suffocating cloud of laughter. A burlap sack of squirming cats hits the water with a splash. And the house where I am sitting at the kitchen table is not a house. My hand seems to be nailed to the wooden tabletop. I am overcome by a feeling of mortal terror. I turn off the burner under the water and rush outside.

The bus snakes its way down the hill into the city. The only other passengers are two old ladies who are speaking animatedly to the driver. I take a deep breath when I notice that the driver is turning his eyes away from the road to look at the ladies as he speaks. His hands rise up off the steering wheel from time to time and he gestures wildly, driving home some point. The bus races along the widening street into the city. We stop between the railroad station and the shopping mall, a huge complex made of red marble. I vividly recall how I came out of that station a year ago, legs wobbly from long sitting. I was at once excited and terrified—I was finally about to meet Lucy. And there was this shopping mall, a gigantic block of red stone glowing in the light of the setting sun, looking for all the world as if it were the source of the accumulated heat of the day. My head was spinning. The white-paved square in front of the mall seemed to have been freshly washed, and though there were many people about, it had an air of desolate emptiness about it.

In a small alley between two close-set rows of houses, I come across the Orion, a little movie theater that smells of raspberry ice cream, popcorn and urine. Three other patrons attend the afternoon show. One of them, a young man with dirty blond hair and a light-green jacket, sits two seats away from me. It's an American movie. On the screen, a man walks into a run-down house. You can hear the cars roaring past on the freeway outside. He puts a bag of groceries down on the table and calls his entire family together. When the kids have stuffed themselves and gone off again, the man jams a piece of steak into his wife's mouth, pushes her back onto the kitchen table and pulls her breasts out of her yellow summer dress. "Not here," she protests with her mouth still full. "The children—"

"Yeah, so?" he says and bites her on the nipple.

"Please," she says and he carries her into the living room and puts her down on the couch. She laughs. Her face is hard but pretty. "Where'd you get the money to buy all that food?" she whispers.

"That was the last of it. They gave me notice today."

She wrenches herself away from him, stamps her feet and lets out a string of curses. The man takes off and rides his motorcycle into town, where he meets up with his buddies in a bar. Later that night he invites them all back to the house, and in the middle of the party, the wife comes down and the fight starts up again. The drunks all flee from the house and roar back into town on their Harleys. Upstairs, while the parents demolish the furniture, the children huddle together in bed, their eyes open wide.

A family walks into the theater carrying ice

cream cones, and just then a bell sounds to indicate intermission. The man beside me pulls a cell phone from his pocket and dials. "This movie's crap," he says and then continues talking, even when the movie starts up again. He doesn't even so much as glance at the screen, where the fight is now coming to a head. He yells. She yells. He punches her and she flies across the living room, landing with a crash against the far wall. She is slumped over, spattered with blood. "Motherfucker," she sputters, and he rips the yellow dress to shreds with his hands.

The guy on the cell phone talks louder and louder over the movie. He looks down at the darkness, where his shoes must be.

"If you have to get a car," he says. "It's got to be one with an airbag. Especially when you think about the children."

I can hear a woman's voice coming from the receiver: "I didn't know you wanted children."

"All right, all right," he responds, putting on a deep voice intended to be soothing. "We'll just have to see, won't we?"

Then he gets up from his seat, shooting me an angry, reproachful look, as if I had been eavesdropping, and bounces out of the theater. I notice that his shoes are mint green.

Outside the theater, I hear the sad melody of an organ grinder coming from down the block. The music makes me like the movie better, and as I approach, I try to imagine the life of the old man who plays it. He turns the crank and keeps a wide, forced smile on his face. Sitting on the organ, which shines like new, is a small, stuffed monkey. A couple of kids are standing nearby eating ice cream and listening to the music. As I walk behind the organ grinder, I notice a CD player lying on the ground—the organ is a fake. I move on quickly and buy myself a scoop of banana ice cream from a cart. Somewhere I've read that bananas make you happy. But the ice cream in my mouth has no flavor to it, it's just sweet and sticky. I dump it in the next trash can.

I pause at the window of a hair salon to look at the barber's chairs. They seem light and airy, though they're actually heavily upholstered. I can't get them out of my head, and a couple of blocks down the street, I turn and go back to the salon. A heavily made-up older woman seats me in one of the cloud chairs and asks me to wait a moment. She disappears behind a narrow door, and I can hear her talking to someone, the way parents do to disobedient children. The she returns with a stack of fashion magazines and shows me every possible haircut, color and permanent. But all I want to do is sit in the cloud, so I just ask for a trim. She spins around and calls, "Mario." A young man appears in the narrow doorway. He slouches through the room with his arms dangling loosely at his sides as if to say he doesn't give a shit about either this salon or the boss lady, who now stands back at the front desk, glancing furtively toward us from time to time. He rolls my chair indifferently over to the sink, and ice-cold water rushes across my scalp. I wonder if the old lady has somehow aggravated him, and he's turned the water on me to get back at her. Perhaps he imagines her head as he grabs roughly at my hair.

When my hair has been washed, he rolls me in front of one of the mirrors. In its reflection, I look through the salon's plate-glass window and see a car driving down the street in double. It drives in my direction, and at the same time its mirror image drives the other way, moving toward a head-on collision. I watch two buses, both jam-packed with passengers, crash silently into one another. The people in the bus windows come face to face with their doubles, merge with them and disappear, as if into some vortex deep in the earth.

The sound of scissors snipping returns me to the salon. Mario is clipping sullenly away at my hair, and it's clear he couldn't care less how it looks when he's done. Then the door flies open and a girl wearing orange sunglasses and carrying a cello case walks in. It's the girl I always see by the equestrian monument in the park.

"Rea!" calls the proprietress, jumping up from behind the counter and pulling out one of the clouds for her to sit in. It seems like Rea is a regular. Even Mario nods at her in the mirror and draws his lips back into a tight smile. Just as I'm thinking it's about time to get up out of my cloud, Mario claps the bonnet of a hair dryer over my head and says it will be another half an hour. I want to ask him *what* exactly will be another half an hour—all I asked for was a trim—but he's already gone, vanished behind the narrow door. The wires and air jets of the hair dryer grow hot, and I strive to keep my head perfectly still so my scalp doesn't get scorched. Out of the corner of my eye, I can see Rea and the old woman, who is rubbing a powerful-smelling chemical mixture into her hair. The dryer roars in my ears, drowning out other sounds, and the woman's mouth appears to snap open and shut without effect. As I watch, the fluid strips the dirty blonde from Rea's hair. She sits there in her cloud with a bright whiteness on top of her head, just like the colorless hair of an old woman.

E V E R Y   E V E N I N G a monk comes out onto the parapet of the monastery and waters the geraniums. The water drips with a quiet patter onto the street beneath, which separates the monastery from our garden. I set a plate of grilled eggplant on the table. Lucy returned today at noon.

She seems rested, as if she's been away somewhere where the air is fresh and the sun shines brightly.

"So, how did you spend the weekend?" she asks me. One of the dark-purple slices of eggplant slips between her painted lips and disappears. She gives off an aroma of sand and salt sea air, and I notice that I am staring at her red fingernails. I picture her painting them in Vito's white-tiled bathroom in the morning light.

"Did you go into the city?"

"No," I lie, because otherwise she'll ask me what I did, and then how the movie was, and I never know how to answer those questions.

"You can't just stay around here the whole time. It's so dreary."

"Why not? It's nice here."

"I really think you should go into the city now and then. You know, I have a car now. Vito lent me one."

After we eat, Lucy wants to show me the car. We walk to a parking lot near the town wall and climb into a large sedan. The inside smells like leather.

The air coming from the A/C is so cold that the fine blond hairs on our arms stand on end. We roll silently down the hill.

"So, will you be seeing a lot of Vito?"

Lucy nods very slightly.

"Seems like he's pretty loaded."

"Actually, Jo, that's none of your business—but he did inherit some money from his uncle recently."

"Hey, great. I guess that means he'll be able to spend a lot of time with you." I am pleased that it comes out sounding so insolent, but Lucy's mouth remains a straight line. It doesn't move. She sits behind the wheel so naturally, as if this had always been her car. It's the first object that she has brought back with her from Vito's world, but I know that soon the house will change, filling up with his gifts. The walls of the house where Alois lived will echo with Lucy and Vito's voices, rising up to the ceiling, and it will seem completely natural, as if it had always been that way.

Lucy drives to the neighboring town, which is nothing but one enormous construction site. We get out and peer through a chain-link fence into an excavation that's maybe fifty feet deep. Workers in yellow jumpsuits are shoveling dirt onto conveyor belts. Backhoes claw at the earth, scoop up great rocks and drop them crashing into the backs of dumptrucks, which drive away with enormous loads. Cement mixers are preparing the foundation for the underground garage of a new hotel. A bunch of children stands next to us, their fingers looped through the mesh of the fence. Their loud voices vie with the construction noise as they make guesses about how long it will take for the hotel to be completed. Lucy has gone back to the car and is fixing her hair in the rearview mirror when I get in. I ask her if this is one of Vito's projects, but she just shrugs as if it doesn't matter and turns the key in the ignition. I want her to keep on driving, to go somewhere we've never been before, but she heads back the same way we came. An impenetrable lightness seems to surround Lucy like a bell jar, and just to shake things up a bit I depress the button that rolls down the window. I think of Lucy's indifferently shrugging shoulders, and suddenly I don't give a shit about anything. I turn and hiss at the side of her face, with no intonation in my voice:

"If you can't say whether it's Vito who's torn down half the village to put up his new hotel, maybe you could at least clear up a few things about Alois. It wasn't an accident, was it? We should really discuss this, at least once. After all, we both know how you lied to Dr. Alberti."

I say it all very fast, and the sentences hang in the air as I utter them. The blood has drained from Lucy's lips. They are colorless except for a few pink crumbs of lipstick and chapped skin at the corners. The car races silently along the curvy road. Beyond the olive trees on the hill, the village wall comes into sight. I watch as it reveals more and more of itself with every yard we travel. Slowly my words sink to the ground. As heavy as steel I-beams, they press me into my seat with their weight and lie there on top of me, crushing me, until we get home and head silently for our separate rooms.

I N M Y dream, Lucy is sitting in a white-tiled bathroom. Her body is strangely bent, and she is painting her toenails. I want to apologize to her for something and reach out my hand, but when it makes contact I find I am touching her naked skull. There is not a single hair on Lucy's head. I call out to my father, who is standing in the corner, but where his mouth should be, there is a row of red crosses. His eyes are crosses too, and when I go to him, he is nothing but a little rag doll that falls into my arms.

I no longer wake screaming when I have nightmares. My sheet is wet with the sweat of fear, and I hang it out the window in the sun. I open all the windows and let the sun in to dry up my dream. I hate my dreams. But at least I no longer wake screaming.

T O D A Y I S Lucy's forty-fifth birthday. I take a tray with breakfast to her room. The sheet is wadded up in a ball in the middle of the bed.

Lucy has told me she thinks that the garden

would look really beautiful if it had a fig tree standing by the steps that lead into it. I take the bus to the outskirts of the next town, where there's a nursery. In a great cement room, trees are lined up in earthenware pots. I stand before a young fig tree. The trunk is spindly, like the emaciated leg of a cripple. Above it, fig leaves reach out on every side.

"Oh, that's a lovely tree," says a saleslady, emerging from the underbrush with a watering can. "It'll be a big one." She sets down the watering can and makes expansive gestures with her arms. "Figs can grow up to thirty feet tall, you know."

She rigs up a cord so I can carry the tree, and I leave with it slung over my shoulder.

On the way back to the bus station, I walk along a tree-lined street with benches set between the trees. I approach two girls sitting together with their heads bent over a book. They are reading aloud from it in whispers, conspiratorially. The book between them is a bridge, like a structure that connects the figures in a large cast-iron sculpture. They are completely engrossed, removed from their surroundings, and don't even raise their heads as I pass by, though I make a point of breathing loudly.

T H E   E A R T H in the garden is dry and crumbly, but the tree stands. It's about as high as a hazel tree and the fruits are small and hard. It is evening, and, although we have not made plans, I feel sure that Lucy will be home soon. I consider the possibility that she may have been held up in a traffic jam. She'll come through the gate within a couple of hours, surely no longer. I'll go to greet her and the next morning early, while I'm still sleeping, she'll come out to the garden, discover the fig, and cry out with pleasure, waking me up. With this thought in my mind, I leave the house.

By the gate I see four boys, maybe twelve years old, coming from the direction of the woods. One of them is carrying a fishing net and the others hold small cardboard boxes out in front of them. Their downcast faces brighten up a bit when they see me, and in an instant they are upon me, blocking my path. One of them opens his box and extends it toward me.

"Would you like to buy a rare, valuable butterfly? We captured them under very dangerous circumstances," he says. The others nod. "You're our first customer. We'll give you a good price. Take your pick."

"But they're dead." There are maybe a dozen butterflies lying in a cluster at one corner of the white cardboard box.

"Yeah? So? They're still valuable. See?" He picks one of them up by the wing and dangles it in front of my nose. The boys draw together, forming a wall, and stare at me, impatient and aggressive because I didn't understand the value of their goods.

"Everyone wants one. They're rare. Nearly extinct!" He is almost yelling now, and I nod and hand over some money. They let me go. When they're out of sight, I chuck the box of dead butterflies into the brush.

I   L E A N up against the village wall, my hands pressed to its warm surface, and wait for Lucy's car to round the bend in the road. She doesn't come, and I gaze down at the houses below, their rooftops prickling with antennas. As night falls, they sink slowly out of sight like ships and are swallowed up by the darkness. I imagine the people who live down there, how they get ready for bed, the way they lay their heads down on fluffy white pillows. And then their faces, crumpled from the long day, open up like the blooms of prehistoric flowers, and their dreams float slowly upward toward the ceiling. Enormous balloons burst against the corners of the furniture that fills their houses. And I think of the never-ending flow of traffic that will soon enough draw the sleepers outside again, into the blue air of the early morning.

•

THE DOORBELL rings, snatching me from a dreamless sleep. I reel down the stairs to the door. The mailman hands me a postcard and a package. The card is from Lucy and bears the postmark of an island in the Indian Ocean. She writes that Vito sprung the trip on her—a big surprise—and she's taking the opportunity to relax completely, for once. I am welcome to have people over to the house, she says. The card does not mention when she will return. The package is from my father, a book, which I put to the side without looking at it. In his letter, he says that he has moved out to the countryside, to the house where Anna and Pauline live, and he gives me his new address. He hopes I'll be back soon and says that of course I am welcome to live with them until school starts and I've found my own apartment. Pauline would love to have me visit. I can't understand how he could write that when he knows that Pauline and I can't stand each other. She's Anna's daughter. We first met at a Christmas dinner to which Anna had invited Father and me. Pauline was thirteen, and we faced each other at the dinner table and checked one another out before exchanging any words. Finally, she asked me if I shaved my legs. I said no. She said she knew a girl who had used a home-waxing kit where you applied the wax to your legs in strips and when you ripped it off all the hair stuck to the wax. But this girl's skin tore off in strips as well, and she ended up in the hospital. Her legs were now hideous with scars. She told the story with a reproachful tone, as if she suspected I had done the same but was too much of a coward to admit it.

After dinner someone asked her to play the piano. She refused in a petulant way that made it clear she *would* play—but only if everyone begged her. They did, and she trotted off to fetch her music. I haven't been back to their house since then, and the idea that, when I return, I will be living with them makes me feel I'm suffocating, gasping at the thin air.

The remote control is on the table. I reach out, push a button on the little black box and turn on the television. There's an ad for an iron that will smooth your clothes perfectly, and it's tiny enough to fit into a lady's handbag, too! Then the phone number you can call if you want to order it. Anti-cellulite massagers, stainless steel pots and pans, fitness machines, bathroom sets. As I watch these ads, I imagine the people who jump up and dial the toll-free numbers. I wish I were one of them, that there was something I needed among all those products.

•

OUTSIDE IT'S ninety-one de-
grees. That's what they said on the radio, anyway.
I'd like to get back into bed and go to sleep, but
the brightness of the day penetrates the house and
convinces me to wait for nightfall. Actually, what
I'd really like would be to go back to the salon and
spend the day with the dryer on my head. Mario
and the old woman would think I was crazy to go
get my hair cut again after only two days. I suppose
I could go and demand a refund for the permanent
that I didn't even ask for, but I ought to have ob-
jected at the time. These things never occur to me
until it's too late.

In the bus on the way to the city, I run through
all the possible scenarios that might lead to my
getting the money back. I won't go through with
any of them. I'm just glad to have something to
think about until it's time to climb down from the
bus and be swallowed up by the city. In the city, I
have to concentrate just to cross the street without
being run down by a truck, just to avoid colliding
with oncoming pedestrians or trampling the little
children who run to and fro, uncontrolled, causing
traffic jams and holding up the orderly flow of bodies along the sidewalk. Old people are the same
way, stumbling out in front of you, all hunched

over, blocking your path. Everywhere there are red and white construction barricades. Enormous steam rollers flatten fresh, steaming tar, while just one block over, the toothy clamshell of a backhoe rips the asphalt up again. The din of the roadwork swallows up the usual sounds of the traffic and the mothers calling out to their children, who skitter about with outstretched arms, as if they had just snapped their tethers. People gush from the shops onto the street in short bursts and whack me on the shins with shopping bags jammed full of hard, sharp objects. In daylight the streets of the city are arteries that threaten to burst, and the people and vehicles that rush along them are riding the flood tide of blood.

It's a broiling hot day. The sun hides behind a thick, gray haze, and beneath it the city gasps like a dying animal striving to fill its lungs with fetid air. Drops of sweat roll slowly from my armpits down along my body, tickling me, and I swear I will give the next person who sidles too close to me a sharp, wrathful elbow in the gut—quite by accident, of course. I am overcome by dizziness and lean up against the plate-glass window of a butcher's shop. Skinned rabbits lie in rows on wide green trays, their feet tucked by their heads as if they were sleeping. The outer surface of their flesh is thin, taut, transparent and covered with a network of fine veins, violet branchings, forks and knots where they intersect. I see a chaos of streets in this dead flesh and smile at myself: how angry, how nasty, I must be to see a parallel between the city and a dead rabbit.

G E T   A W A Y from that window!" shrieks a lady who has just stuck her head out of the butcher shop. "You're *not* allowed to *lean* on the window!"

The street continues on past cheap jewelry shops and the skeletons of houses that are just going up. In front of the construction site, two gangs of kids bait each other. This street leads to the square with the equestrian monument, where a small group of people has gathered in a semicircle around Rea. They crane their heads forward because she is playing almost too quietly to hear. She's got her bleached-out hair piled up on top of her head, and a few strands fall in front of her eyes, which are hidden behind the orange lenses of her sunglasses. I wonder why the hell a person would wear sunglasses all the time, even when the sun wasn't shining. I wait till the people have cleared away and I am standing alone in front of her. Rea jumps up from her folding chair and collects the money from her cello case. I try to sound friendly, but I can't conceal my annoyance when I say, "If it's not sunny, shouldn't you actually be wearing *blue* sunglasses?"

"No. Orange lasts longer." She responds without looking at me, still bent over the cello case. Then she snaps the clasps shut and takes off her glasses.

"It takes a while to get used to seeing everything in orange. With these it took me two weeks." She looks down at the glasses as if they were an object of great value. "We've met before, you know —at the salon. We sat next to each other." She is squinting at me. I find this unpleasant, as I've been watching her all this time with the idea that she'd never noticed my presence. She puts her sunglasses back on, picks up her cello and looks at me quizzically. "I'm going to get something to eat. Come along if you want. You look like you're about to keel over, you know."

We go off together without talking. It's odd the way two strangers can walk down the street beside each other so naturally. Rea's hair doesn't even flutter slightly when she moves, and I have a strong desire to touch it with my hand, to see if it's as stiff as it looks. She heads for a restaurant near the train station. We walk into a deserted room with white tablecloths on the tables. Thick folded linen napkins perch in front of us at our table like birds about to take flight. We are the only patrons. Three waiters look at us expectantly from behind a shiny chrome counter, but it takes several minutes before one of them emerges into the main room to take our order.

"So, let me guess—you're not from here," Rea says, pursing her lips ironically. I keep getting the feeling I know her from somewhere. I explain to her how I came here the previous summer, after I finished school, to visit my mother. And how her husband, my stepfather, was killed in an accident after I arrived, and how my mother got sick afterward and how I therefore felt that I had to stay around until she was better.

"So what's she doing right now?"

"She's at home," I lie. "She's always at home. Since the accident she's completely terrified of cars and going out on the street and groups of people. She spends the whole time sitting in her garden talking to her lilies." Then I tell her how Lucy turned Alois's studio into a pollen room after the accident and locked herself in and how I finally rescued her.

"So, is she doing better?"

"Oh, yeah, a lot better really. I'll be really glad when I can get the hell out of here. This is a hideous city," I say, even though we live on the outskirts, in a village at the top of a hill.

"Yeah, everywhere is," she says with a disgusted flick of the wrist.

"What?"

"*Hideous.* Everywhere is hideous."

Rea talks fast and snappy and mostly in catch-phrases.

"Are you studying music at the conservatory?" I ask, casting a glance at the cello. When the waiter brings us our soup, Rea unfolds her napkin, tucks it into the neck of her shirt, and leans over her bowl so that the tip of the linen bird's wing dips into the broth. "No," she says. "That's what my parents want me to do. Actually, I don't do anything. They said that if I didn't want to go to university and didn't want to work, I should play cello. Of course they never meant I should be a street musician. You can't imagine how it drives them crazy." She takes a deep breath, as if drawing the energy to continue speaking from the air.

"But now they've got other things to worry about. It's a total joke to think that I'm going to be a millionaire when they die. Real estate holdings, stocks, fancy houses, they've got everything."

When Rea leans back in her chair, the tip of the napkin emerges from the bowl, pinkish and soaked with soup. She flashes a crooked smile, and I realize that she reminds me of some cartoon character I've seen.

F O R A long time the night had no end. During the countless hours that I lay awake, I found myself completely unable to recall the day. The darkness was forever. Now I can sleep because I know that when I open my eyes again, morning will be there. But daylight no longer gives me the feeling of salvation. Quite the opposite. It's the light that tortures me now. When I ride the bus back home from the city, I'm surprised to find myself squinting the whole way. The sun is nowhere to be seen, but the light falls on every object like a spotlight. The air is different too. It hangs over the city like a burden, and I have to breathe through my mouth because my nose is stuffed up. Sitting in the bus, I blow black snot into my handkerchief. The light is so harsh that my eyes begin to water. I can't stop rubbing my eyes. Everyone else does it too, rubbing their eyes as if it were the most natural thing in the world, like swatting away a fly or scratching an itch. Everyone seems exhausted, depleted, trudging around with red, swollen lids.

REA'S FATHER is a successful genetic engineer. He owns an estate somewhat outside of the city. To approach the house you must pass between two rows of poplars that loom over the gravel driveway like armed guards. The house has four stories, and on every landing there are big-bellied porcelain vases full of artificial flowers.

On the top floor, near Rea's room, is the library. The room has no windows, but in the center of the coffered wooden ceiling, a skylight of milky glass casts muted daylight down onto a round table.

"Do you all ever sit in here together and read?" I ask her, standing before the high shelves.

"What? No. No one ever sits in here," says Rea impatiently from the doorway, her hand on the knob. I look up to the top shelf, which reaches almost to the ceiling and holds a row of leather-bound volumes. I remember the smell of the freshly printed pages, still warm, as they fell in a stack from the rollers of the rumbling old printing press.

We live from books, Father once told me as we ran to the post office together on a winter afternoon to send off an important shipment. The snowflakes stung our faces like tiny arrows, and the corners of the boxes banged against our legs. The freezing wind whisked our breath away in tiny white clouds. I concentrated on my feet, keeping them from stumbling under me.

Whatever you do, I told myself, don't trip. Don't let those packages go flying into the street. That's our livelihood you're carrying. Don't lose your footing on the slippery ice and ruin it all. One foot beside the other, run, but not too fast, and don't fall behind, and don't fall down!

"They're all antiquarian volumes, inherited. Some of them are really valuable. Nobody's ever even taken one down, much less read them." Rea is behind me all of a sudden and herds me out of the library. Her room is decorated with a bright-blue wallpaper and a high bedstead with rounded edges and a TV that looks like a coffin.

"Just so you know," says Rea, standing in front of the window, "this is really my parents' room, not mine. I would never tolerate such wallpaper in my own room. What I mean is, my mother is responsible for the interior decorating." Then she shows me her video collection, which is enormous. They're stacked up in a chest beside the bed, and each one has a number written on it. She shows me how the numbers are recorded in a register.

"My mother. She's so organized it's psychotic."

We plop down on the bed and lean up against the big cushions. Rea puts on her favorite movies, one after another. The thrillers make her so nervous that she's constantly hitting fast forward, and the scenes race by on the screen. We bite our nails and scoot closer and closer together on the bed, holding hands that are clammy with terror.

"You want to see something totally cool?" she asks, going to the cabinet and pulling out another tape. *Apocalypse Now*. She goes straight to the end, where the napalm bombs fall into the jungle like comets from the night sky. Then the earth explodes all at once and palm trees go flying through the air, light as feathers, and land in the river. The black water mirrors the fire raging on the bank in a wild dance of glittering spray. "A perfect fireworks show," says Rea, and then she hits rewind.

I N C H E S F R O M my head a pink dome rises up—Rea's heel, the first thing I see upon waking. Then her leg twitches in her sleep and the foot zooms toward my face. I roll off the edge of the bed to the floor to evade it. We have both fallen asleep in our clothes. A black-and-white snowstorm rages on the television screen. Rea snorts quietly, her face buried in one of the pillows. She is dreaming. I turn off the TV and get up to open the window. A warm breezes wafts in against my face. Directly beneath the window is a swimming pool shaped like a fish. The floor of the pool is covered with mosaic tiles depicting Neptune with his trident. I look out to the light-green hills that rise behind the trees and stretch across the horizon. Rea told me that besides her and her parents, a gardener, a housekeeper and a cook live in this house, but on this morning everything is quiet. It seems to me it would be possible to pass one's entire life in this house without ever seeing another person. Only Neptune would be there all the time. All at once I find it terribly strange, the way he lies there motionless beneath the water, and I imagine that in

Rea's childhood dreams he rose up out of the pool, ascended to her window and pointed his trident in the direction of her bed. Had she cried out, there would have been no one to hear it.

"So, is it still summer out?" Rea is sitting up in bed with swollen eyes. "Because, if it is, we should go swimming. My parents built the pool for me, but most of the time I'm alone and I'd rather stay in my room."

She crawls around on the bed looking for her sunglasses and, when she finds them, gets up and goes to the chifforobe.

"Pick one!" She tosses a dozen bathing suits out onto the floor. As I rummage indecisively through the pile of suits, Rea emerges from behind the tall door in a bikini with red and yellow flowers. Her nipples poke high and straight through the fabric. Our bare feet vanish without a trace in the deep, fluffy carpet the same color blue as the wallpaper.

Still barefoot, we go down the four stories to the ground level, pass through a long corridor that leads to a room with pictures of water lilies on the wall and beige upholstered chairs. On a side table stands a small glass vase from Murano and, beside it, a framed photograph. It is Rea, maybe six years old and in pigtails, sitting with her cello and gazing with concentration at the floor.

"Oh, I hate that one!" Rea grabs the picture out of my hand and places it face down on the table. "They had big plans for me. Can't you just imagine how it drove them crazy when they found out I was going to become a street musician in the city? I showed them," she says and slides the glass door open.

We carry an umbrella and two lounge chairs from an equipment shed to the side of the pool. We stretch our legs out in front of us on the blue-and-white-striped chairs.

"When my parents are gone, all this will be mine."

"Gone where?"

"When they're dead."

Under the umbrella, little blotches of reflected light and dark prongs of shadow dance across our bellies. The flowers on Rea's bikini flash in the sun like traffic lights. She slowly massages coconut oil into the flesh of her thighs.

"So, do you have a boyfriend?" she asks. The lenses of her sunglasses gaze at me like the eyes of a dangerous tropical lizard.

"No."

"Ever had one?"

"Oh, yeah, sure, a long time ago." I decide I should really shut up, but the next question is already taking form on Rea's lips, so I plunge ahead.

"Actually, he's dead. He drowned. He got pulled out by the tide in the Indian Ocean and was never seen again."

"Far out." Rea stretches out the words into impossibly many syllables.

I can hardly believe I made up such a ridiculous story to tell her. I picture him being swept away into the sea, his head and arms a small white triangle growing smaller and smaller until all I can see is a tiny spot, the hair on the top of his head, sinking beneath the waves.

T H E   P A R T Y was thrown by my father's much younger girlfriend in the rear courtyard of her apartment building. Father knew that I was in the habit of eating next to nothing all day long, and he made me promise I would go and stuff myself. She was ten years younger than Father, in fact, and he also thought it would be fun for me to hang out with people closer to my age. The building's entranceway was cluttered with bikes and opened into a courtyard surrounded by high walls. There was a bunch of kids standing around on the gravel drinking wine out of plastic cups. Food was laid out on a long table, and the voice of Laurie Anderson blared from an open window in the building above. I made my way through the crowds of people to the table, took a plate from the stack and proceeded to pile it as high as I could with food. Unfortunately Father's girlfriend happened to spot me just as I was tackling a large pie. The piece I had cut was stuck to the knife and I was having the damnedest time getting it off. She strode slowly over to me and introduced me all around to the partygoers, in a loud voice. "This is my boyfriend's daughter," she said, obviously pleased to have living proof that she was dating a man much older than herself. She clearly found it a highly desirable affiliation, but Father never went to her parties, and her friends probably doubted his existence. Having me there seemed to be a real triumph for her, especially with the women.

It was a mild spring evening, and a linden tree was blooming in a neighboring yard. The wind blew the linden blossoms over the wall and the air was thick with them, like confetti.

For some time now I'd had a mental image of the man I could love. He had to be just like D.B., the protagonist of a novel that I'd read approximately twenty times at that point. I knew just how he looked, how he smoked, how he moved. Every man I met, I compared with this fictional character, and it hadn't taken long to figure out that there was no one like D.B in the entire town.

THERE WAS a guy leaning up against the wall, awkwardly, looking as if he'd been nailed to it. Someone was standing next to him, talking to him, but he didn't even bother to look. Under his black eyebrows, which fused into one at the bridge of his nose, his eyes darted this way and that. At last they strayed across mine, and his gaze seemed grasp onto me. It was clear that he had nothing to do with this other person. He wasn't much to look at, really—he looked like someone on the run. But it was the first time I had ever felt drawn to an actual living person, as if some force had taken control over my body. I continued staring at the place against the wall where he had stood, even after he was standing next to me, talking. He said he was into experimenting with computer music, he was right in the middle of inventing something totally new. I didn't care what he said. I was too busy staring at the ropy blue veins on his white arms. The throb of his pulse was visible beneath the skin.

I came upon my father's girlfriend squatting in a flower bed embracing a drunken man who was trying to kiss her neck. When she saw me, she waved, pressed her lips together and rolled her eyes as if this was just a silly little episode, certainly not worth mentioning to my father. The plastic cup of red wine grew warm in my hand. A linden blossom floated through the air, spinning like a propeller, and landed in my cup. I was about to laugh, but then the guy came and took the cup from me. He said there was no point in hanging around at a party where you had to drink wine out of plastic cups. I agreed, and before I knew it, we had left the courtyard and were walking along the street. It made me fairly sick to be walking so close to him, as if we were together. My mind was blank, empty of all thoughts.

The parquet floors in his apartment were old and creaked with every step. There were hundreds of CDs in rows against the wall, and an enormous stereo system towered in the corner with cables and microphones snaking out onto the floor. It was suddenly not clear to me what I was doing in this room. I wanted to ask him if maybe we could get together some other time, but his arms were already upon me. They lifted me weightlessly from the floor. He carried me to a mattress in another room and undressed me. His face loomed above me, horrible and unfamiliar. I saw him in fragments—his chin, his nose—strange and magnified, as if through a jeweler's glass. I would have liked to push all the pieces away from me, but instead I stared at the ceiling and held my breath. I saw a rust-brown water spot like a great amoeba. I heard a sound coming from the ceiling, as if a ball were rolling across the floor in the apartment above. My eyes followed the noise as the ball rolled across the water spot and then landed with a crash against the wall. Something was whispering in my ear, but I couldn't make it out, so focused was I on the strange noises from above. My arm lay on the mattress in a painful, unnatural position, as if it had been trampled.

He fell fast asleep as soon as he lay down beside me. I could tell from his breathing and the heaviness and stillness of his body next to mine. I pulled my leg out from under his and rolled away so we weren't touching. I had the sudden feeling of having forgotten something important. I thought of the movie about AIDS they'd shown us in school. The credits indicated which of the subjects had died during the post-production with a little superscripted cross. One of them was a nineteen-year-old guy. Just a few minutes before we'd seen him talking onscreen about how he wanted to be a dancer. He was completely convinced that his energy level and strength would enable him to overcome the disease. Then he leapt up and began pirouetting across the room, spinning like a dervish and cutting capers that transformed the room into a stage for a few brief minutes.

He proudly showed off the offers he'd received to dance with international companies. The letters trembled in his hands, and he looked into the camera with an unbelievably wide smile across his lips, as if to say, See, I'm standing here right on the verge of something great. How could I be deathly ill? You don't believe it either, do you?

The teacher turned on the lights and waved the class out to recess, leaving us upset by the movie and furious with him for having shown it to us, for having burdened us in that way. We slunk out of the classroom with shuffling steps while he, the destroyer, remained behind.

I looked down at my body—which would, perhaps, soon be dead—thought about the dancer and felt a terror that ached in every part of me. It overflowed me and ran out onto the sheets where I lay.

I sat up in bed and shook him. I was desperate to talk to him, but he wouldn't wake up. I ran to the shower and made the water so hot that it burned my skin, imagining that I could somehow destroy the virus this way. I stopped up my ears and heard the blood roaring, saw the rush of blood before my eyes and the viruses, small jagged-edged balls that burst open, multiplied and deceptively rushed along with the flow, only to one day bring the churning of the blood to a halt. I decided that this guy was nothing like D.B. after all and lost every desire to be swept up in his arms. It was so like me not to remember the essential thing until it was too late. By the time I got out of the shower my skin was glowing red and crawling, as if thousands of ants were walking across it. I took the bed covers off of him, went into the other room and lay down on the floor beside the stereo tower.

A flash of light wrenched me back into the room from my deep slumber.

"Good morning, my sleeping angel," he said, grinning and brandishing a Polaroid camera above me.

I looked up into his unfamiliar features with rage.

"You're going to have to get an AIDS test," I told him and ripped the picture from his hand.

"Jesus Christ, so now you're going be rational all the sudden?"

He was offended, but he went off to find a piece of paper and tossed it at me. The address of a hospital at the top and check mark next to the word *negative.*

I heard him whistling in the kitchen and smelled coffee brewing as I slipped out the front door.

Two months later, I lay on my back, my feet up in stirrups. I heard the word *Rhohypnol,* and it echoed inside my head, growing ever larger. Over and over, *Rhohypnol,* until I slipped away into the word and sank out of sight.

When I awoke after the abortion, I found myself under a white blanket, my eyes blinking at a beam of light that shone through a gap in the curtains and landed on a strip of green floor tile. Bright motes of dust swirled through it like tiny flashbulbs going off. Someone came into the room. A great light creature pulled a chair up to the bed and took my hand, which was cold and damp with sweat. He spoke to me, but I would not look my father in the eye. From where I lay, I examined the dust in the beam of light and felt myself rolling away like a ball of polished lead.

INSIDE THE house the telephone rings.

"Aren't you going to get it?"

She shakes her head. "It's just the old lady."

"You're not going to get it?"

"Why should I? She's just going to want me to come visit her."

"Is she away?"

"Yeah, she's fucking *away*. She's in the hospital, okay? She's got cancer. She's dying."

The telephone doesn't stop ringing.

"And she wants me to watch while she does it. Yeah, well, she can watch *me* for once, you know?" Her voice rises and she goes on. "Dad should be the one who visits her, but no, he's constantly off at some conference or other. He doesn't even seem to have noticed that his wife is on her deathbed."

"Oh, man, that's like so—I mean, I'm really sorry about your mom," I sputter, but Rea just says, in a singsong voice, "Whatever," and waves her hand in the air as if swatting away a great swarm of flies.

When the phone stops ringing, she goes inside and brings out a transparent telephone. The vari-colored wires are visible through the plastic. She calls up a friend of hers, Nicola. He's a total wacko, she tells me. And a half an hour later he's standing there, with his arm around Rea. He kisses me too, with his hard, thin lips. Rea leaps into the pool. Nicola goes over to a little control panel mounted at the edge of the pool, pushes a button, and waves rise up in the water. He sits on the edge of the pool and dangles his feet in the water.

"I'm gonna throw you in! I'm gonna throw you in!" cries Rea, but the current is so strong that she can't make her way forward, no matter how hard she swims. After a while, when she gets a little bit closer and reaches up her hand to grab him, the current drags her back a yard and she flails in the water with her arms. Neptune wobbles and slithers beneath her like a snake, dividing into two and coming back together again. Nicola grins mali-ciously and kicks his foot in the water. He's wearing baggy shorts that go down to his knees and a T-shirt that says GET INTO AN AIRPLANE WHILE YOU STILL CAN. After a while, Rea goes to the side of the pool and climbs out, red in the face. The fabric of her bikini is dark with the wet and the flowers hang dripping from her breasts. Her hair looks like straw. Big drops of water fall from it. I wonder if the lady at the salon has inadvertently ruined it. Nicola jumps up from the side of the pool and sits himself down between our two lounge chairs.

"So, I'm going to this techno party tonight. You can come if you want. I've got Ecstasy."

Rea dries her sunglasses on her towel. Her little blue eyes flash at me. "Check it out. He wants to turn us into drug addicts—the evil Nicola!" She punches him jokingly in the neck.

"No, really, not this time, Nicola," she says at last. "It always makes me feel like hell for days afterward."

N I C O L A   T E L L S us to wait in the car until he's changed for the party. He goes into one of the concrete buildings past the playground. They stand close enough together to form a single great wall. The playground is nothing but a pit full of black sand and a rusty old jungle gym. Two boys are swinging from it lazily, seeming to sway lightly in the breeze. They're pretty young, but their foreheads are covered with pimples. When they see us, they drop heavily into the sand and stand there staring as if we were their enemies. Then they give us the finger.

"Oh, my God, aren't children charming," Rea says in exaggerated tones. "I'm planning to go out and have a whole bunch of them." She shakes her head disgustedly as they crouch down and begin to form balls of dirt and black sand in their palms and lob them at us. Suddenly Rea throws open the car door, raises her fist, and screams so loud that I cringe in my seat and the two boys jump in the air.

"Go fuck off, you little shits!"

At first they run, terrified, a few yards across the lawn, then turn back and look at us with wide-open eyes as if they had just been dragged from deepest slumber, except that they are also defiant and full of loathing. Then they run off together without turning back again and go into one of the buildings like animals retreating to their dens. By the time Nicola returns, night has fallen. He's wearing a white jumpsuit and glacier goggles that cover half his face. It seems like it's gotten dark all at once, with no transition, no sunset, no twilight. We cruise down the highway passing factory buildings that stand empty like haunted houses.

It's a clear, starry night. Rea sticks her head out the window and says, "I've never seen a comet. You know, I'd really like to see a comet once." She speaks with the voice of a petulant little girl, and her plastic flower earrings bob up and down like Christmas tree ornaments.

"Maybe if you took off your sunglasses you'd see one," says Nicola, laughing and grinning at me in the rearview mirror. His outfit makes him look like an astronaut.

"You don't understand anything," Rea says and cranks up the window, clearly offended. I squirm in my seat and scratch myself with both hands because the synthetic dress that Rea has lent me for the party feels worse against my skin than wool.

"I'm just going to make a friendly offer," Nicola says, holding out his open hand. There are three small tablets. "Whoever wants can have." I automatically take one and pop it in my mouth, let it dissolve on my tongue. I had expected something sweet, but the taste is both bitter and sour, and I spit the rest into a tissue and let it fall between the seats. Stupidly, I've let Nicola see me do it in the rearview mirror. I feel my face turn red and wait for him to say something, but he doesn't, just watches me. I press myself into the seat and scrunch over to the farthest edge, but his eyes follow my every movement. Even after I turn my face to look out the window I can feel his gaze on the back of my head, all the way to the gravel parking lot in front of the big brick building where we pull up.

From inside the building comes a low, loud, fast thumping. Rea's wearing a green miniskirt and a yellow T-shirt that glows in the dark. I follow her high-laced boots to the entrance. Above the door there's a sign reading HIDE IN PLAIN SIGHT.

Inside, the heat is tropical, and the room

where people are dancing is so thick with dry-ice fog that I lose my orientation completely.

"It's a slaughterhouse!" screams Rea and points up at the ceiling from which great meat hooks still dangle. The bodies of countless animals have hung there. "You are the greatest ravers on the planet!" calls the DJ into his microphone. He's running agitatedly back and forth across a small raised platform illuminated with blinking colored lights. He's got butterfly wings painted on his cheeks. The flow of sounds the butterfly man sends down on upon us percolates in my stomach like a thousand gum balls. The strobe lights flash, and all I can see is detached body parts flying through the space. Rea's arms and legs must be among them but I don't recognize her anymore. I, too, am a part of this enormous machine made of bodies that shake and rear up and generate an hysterical din in an attempt to counteract the terrible silence of the mind. Behind me someone one blows a shrill whistle. As I attempt to turn around, two hands grasp me and tighten around my belly. I look down at them. They are male hands. A body in a plastic suit presses against me like a fish. He shouts something into my ear, but I can't hear him and bite his pierced earlobe. The metal tastes like cold milk. I keep the earring in my mouth for a while, until Rea clomps over and extracts me from the man's grip. By the exit we lean up against the wall together.

"Let's get out of here," she says. "This music is killing me, and I can't dance without Ecstasy."

As we're leaving, the guy appears before us. It looks like his earlobe is still wet. He raises his arms and lets them fall. The irises of his eyes roll around like they're about to jump free. Rea opens up her little pocketbook and pulls out a pacifier, sticks it in the guy's mouth. Then he goes off, sucking between the flashes of the strobe. We stand blind and deaf in the parking lot, expelled into the night by the vast noise machine.

"What about Nicola?" I ask, following in Rea's rapid footsteps.

"We're ditching him. I've got his keys. He'll be too wasted even to find his car by the end of the party." She unlocks the doors.

When we get in I notice the chain that hangs from Nicola's rearview mirror, a small locket swinging at the end of it. I open it and see a photograph if a woman. "Look at that," I say, and Rea takes it in her hand.

"Must be his mother," she says. "To bring him luck if he has an accident and goes flying through the windshield."

I ask Rea if she and Nicola are going out, if they're a couple, but she just shrugs.

"Sex is totally uncool, you know," she says. "I don't know anyone who actually likes it. They all lie about it, you know?"

I don't know what to say to that, so I giggle stupidly, imagining that while Rea and Nicola are doing it in the pool, Neptune cracks a hideous grimace and pokes them in their asses with his trident. Rea gets off the highway and takes a small, paved road through the woods to a rest area with picnic tables, benches and trash barrels. Farther off stands a row of mausoleums. In one of the tombs I see the flickering light of a candle. Rea rolls the window down and leans out to get a better view.

"Wow, man. There's somebody in there," Rea announces, and just then there's a movement, and a little feltlike tuft of hair that had been sticking out of the entranceway vanishes like the head of a frightened turtle. Bottles and old newspapers lie discarded around the tomb. Behind the glass of the windshield, which is flecked with dead bugs, the moon shines in a great white circle. There must be other places than this one, I think, completely different. In our classroom at school there was a map of the world. Time and again, I studied it, pondering those white, green and blue shapes, points of land and meandering lines and outcroppings. I knew early on that that map was a lie, because the true earth had a very different appearance. The geography teacher took great pains as he pointed his stick at various places on the map, always making it seem there was some great secret lurking there, and that we would be the ones to reveal it. From time to time a fleeting, tortured smile would scurry across his lips, letting us all in on the fact that we lived on a planet that was more or less destroyed already and which no one really wanted anymore.

A shadowy image of Rea is reflected in the windshield. Her skin is translucent like the glass. Suddenly I am seized with a dread that she will die young.

"Let's get out of here, Rea." I say. "Let's go to another country."

"Where to? There's nowhere else to go." She shakes her head coldly.

"How do you know that? What about Milwaukee? You've heard of it, right? But you'd probably say no one even lives there."

"Mil-wau-kee." She rolls the word around in her mouth like a morsel of food she has been asked to judge in a taste test.

"I'm going to have to put my mother in a home anyway," I say. "We could go anytime."

I imagine how Rea and I would drive my mentally disturbed mother to a clinic on a warm day with clouds sitting high in the sky. A nurse would take Lucy by the elbow and lead her down a long corridor to her room. She would look back at us with devastated eyes that said, Why are you doing this? Why are you leaving me in this place?

"It will be better this way," I would call to her

ever-diminishing figure, and I would be certain that I was right.

"Yeah, why don't we just have ourselves launched into space and go live on the moon?" Rea is suddenly excited. She looks around and presses her nose to the windscreen to see the moon more clearly. "Imagine it—just us two. And we could send postcards back to the people on earth, saying, Weather's quite cold up here, but we love the life-style. The children are all happy and jump around in the craters. Sometimes we tie them to strings and let them float through the universe like balloons. In the evenings we sit on the hills and look down at you on earth. From this vantage point, the earth looks fragile, and perhaps you should really look into alternative options. Unfortunately though, there's no room left for anyone else up here."

In my dream, the moon is nearly risen, and I hear Rea shivering. She curls up her legs on the chair and rests her head on her knees. It has begun to rain. The light of the candle in the mausoleum grows dimmer and dimmer. The parking lot is a shiny black rectangle. I hope that none of the dead people's families will come to visit them over the weekend. The children would stumble upon the bum who sleeps under the rooftop of the mauso-leum. They would pull his hair and do what they could to roust him while their parents sat on benches and put sausages on to grill, not stopping them. On the contrary, they would take up their skewers and wave them in the air like flags, egging the children on with laughter and cheers.

Dead bugs slide down the windshield slowly, one after another. Rea mumbles, half-asleep, "Don't drive away. The parking lot might be the maw of a giant beast that will snap shut as soon as we try to escape."

S I N C E   L U C Y went away, the garden has grown up feverishly. The plants have already overgrown the little paths. They exude a perfume so rich I think it will suffocate me. That's why I keep the windows closed. At night I can see the scorpions creep out from crevices in the wooden ceiling as if from the void and crawl across the white walls. They go so slowly that they hardly move at all, and I can go two or three hours without looking at them and still find them in the same places. It's when they're gone that I panic, searching the bed and shaking out the clothes on the stool. Where are you? I call. Come back! But it's ridiculous. I've never found a scorpion in my clothes. Probably they just creep right back into the ceiling. I imagine what it's like up there, amongst the rafters, where the scorpions live—maybe hundreds of them. They do everything—feed, sleep and copulate—directly over my head, and now and then one of them decides to take a stroll across my walls. Maybe they come out just to observe me, then go back and report to the others what they've seen and make plans for the great attack when all of them will pour out of the ceiling at once and overcome me.

It's a stupid daydream that has no purpose except to frighten me, but I'm capable of believing such things.

I lie in bed, hungry, and imagine that I'm eating the food that's actually still downstairs in the kitchen. Whenever I cross the threshold of my room, Alois glares at me from the walls, watching me as I move through his house. The house is once again completely his, and I become a thief when I walk down its halls. At last I venture downstairs timidly, like a rabbit at gunpoint, keeping my eyes to the floor. I carry my food back upstairs on a tray, close the door and take the tray into bed with me. I am determined to chew my food very slowly and enjoy every bite of it. Lately I've been wolfing down my food, and afterward there's a dull emptiness in my mouth. I tell myself that I won't eat again for a long, long time; this may even be my very last meal.

THE HOTEL in the next town has been completed, and it towers over the poplars. Men are raised high in the air by a crane to mount the enormous lighted letters for the name on its side: NOVA PARK HOTEL. The letters sway in the air as they are hoisted up on ropes.

The sun shines into the room, right into my eyes. My finger is a beam that I lay across my eyes to block out the light. When I move it even slightly to the side, rainbow-colored circles and ellipses swim out in front of the darkness. The rays of the sun pierce my eyes like needles when I let my finger stray far enough for the light to encounter my retina. Quickly I restore my finger blindfold to its place and don't take it away again.

T H E E M P T Y dining room of the restaurant spreads out before me like a vast sea, and I sit myself down abruptly at a table close to the shore with my back to the wall, as if I am afraid of drowning. The waiters mill around behind the bar, impatiently awaiting the guests who ought to be filling the tables but are, in fact, nowhere in sight. Then the door flies open, and Rea walks in. The waiters watch, curious and alarmed, as she stamps across the room in her combat boots and short flippy skirt holding a bloody handkerchief pressed up against her nose. She sits down at the table without saying hello and calls over to the bar in a husky, mannish voice for a whiskey. The waiters all spring into action to fulfill her request and end up running into one another.

"That pig." I hear her muffled voice coming from under the handkerchief. "I just ran into Nicola," she says. "The other morning, after the party, you know? I drove Nicola's car over to his place and threw the keys through the mail slot. So he's walking along with me for a bit and just as we get to the park he grabs me by the hair and drags me toward him and tells me to beg him for forgiveness. Apparently he had to hitchhike home the next morning. I pulled myself away and told him he was living in the wrong century. I'm supposed to apologize to him? Fuck that." Rea snorts and slams her fist on the table. "I've never apologized for anything in my entire life. Then he tried to grab me again, so I ran, right across the lawn, until I could hear his breath coming up behind me. Then I turned, sprang on him, knocked him down and pinned him. His mouth was going open, shut, open, shut, like a fish out of water. He tried to punch me in the face but I had my knee pressed so hard into his arm that he couldn't move. You know what he said?"

Rea bites down on her handkerchief and sneers.

"He said, *I hate you.*" Rea leans back in her chair triumphantly. "I could feel his legs kicking beneath me as I squeezed his throat. His face went purple when I released him. I grabbed my jeans jacket from the ground where it was lying and walked out of the park past a couple of people who were gawking at Nicola as he lay there, gasping for breath on the grass."

Rea drinks the whiskey down in one gulp.

"I nearly strangled him. It would have been cool if someone was filming it, though. The whole thing would have made a really great ad for a jeans jacket," she says and opens up her purse, dropping the soiled handkerchief into it with her fingertips.

G R A Y   S T R E A K S of cloud cover up the sun. She stamps, my high heels clatter, we hold hands, and I wish that some of Rea's energy would flow over into me.

"Listen, Rea," I say. "Tomorrow I'm taking my mother to the home. You want to get the tickets to Milwaukee or what?"

She nods. She knows a travel agency in the suburbs. On the way there, we pass through the underground city. The hectic voices of addicts emanate from one of the dim corners where they gather. A couple of tourists stand at the roped-off area in front of the skeleton, half-heartedly trying to decipher the information on the plaque, which someone has spray-painted red. Further on we come across a man sitting crouched over on one of the stones. His head hangs down like a useless, heavy object with no connection to the rest of his body.

"What's wrong with him?" I say and stand staring.

"He's just resting, can't you see?"

"He looks dead to me."

"Yeah, well, if he is we might as well leave him in peace. The maintenance crew will find him eventually." Rea pulls on my arm and rushes up an exit I'm not familiar with. Her fingers grip my arm, and she doesn't let go until we're on the escalator. It spits us out into a great black wasteland. In front of us stretches a freshly paved square, and the air is still heavy with the acrid smell of tar. A semicircle of shiny guardrail leads the way to the highway on-ramp. A bus waits, lonely at the curb. Without speaking or even glancing at each other, we run to the bus, both of us seized with a terror that it will drive off without us, stranding us here. In the bus, our naked thighs stick to the warm plastic seats. Kate Moss looks down at us from an advertising poster with a hostile smile. As the city slides past the windows, I think over whether to leave Lucy a note. Why should I? She doesn't care if I'm here or not. This thought bursts in my brain like a water balloon. More and more people board the bus, and we are squeezed up against the window. It seems like the entire population of the city has decided to take this particular bus. As people reluctantly press closer together, the glimmer of the mass murderer steals into their eyes. After a while, Rea pinches me on the arm and whispers, "Our stop's next." I look down at my big toe, which is sticking out of a hole in my shoe. Under the nail, a rind of dirt has collected, turning it into a repulsive landscape in black and white.

We go silently through the streets. The people here have window boxes and potted plants in front of their houses, and little children squat in the front yards and gape at us over hedges as if they were deaf-mutes who had never seen anyone walk down their street before. We walk through a market square, at the very center of which stands a strange round building, as if it were on exhibit. An automatic toilet. I put a coin in the slot and enter the bright, shiny room. A pop tune plays softly from an invisible loudspeaker. I have the feeling I have wandered into a trap and hurry to get out of there as quickly as possible. The wash basin is made of chrome and reflects my face as if it were a rubber mask turned inside out. I look all around for a faucet to turn on the water and wash my hands. There isn't one. Then it suddenly turns on by itself, and I look around, startled, for the camera that must be monitoring my activities. But there's nothing in here other than pale yellow molded plastic. I'm ready to leave, but I can't find a door knob anywhere. I stand before the yellow wall. At the bottom, a thin sliver of sunlight shines through from outside, and I lean down and put my ear to the crack. I can hear the noise of the traffic outside as if from a distance. I stand back up and begin muttering to myself nonsensically. "Okay, just don't panic. It'll open up by itself eventually." Then the pop song is interrupted abruptly and there's a noise from inside the walls. "Something's wrong," I scream and then cringe when I realize how loud I just was. But when the toilet still doesn't open up, I start to yell in earnest, at the walls. All I can hear is my own voice, and I'm yelling so loud without stopping to breathe that soon I'm dizzy. At last, the walls part with a buzzing sound, and I stumble out onto the empty square. I look at the roofs and the houses and walk toward the newsstand where Rea is leafing through a paper. She buys a whole pile of papers and magazines for our trip. A couple of blocks later we come to the travel agency, but it's locked up. The little sign in the window with the hours indicates that it ought to be open now, and Rea curses and presses her nose up against the glass. Inside, it is dark. Rea says it doesn't matter, she'll just buy the tickets over the telephone, and we turn and make our way back to the bus station. Since we set out, the gray clouds have spread themselves over the entire expanse of sky. Thunder comes faintly from far away. Two little girls jump down from a swing set and run into a house. The rain comes fast and hard. Drops the size of grapes smash against our bodies, and there are no shops, no restaurants, anywhere in sight for us to duck into. We run along a street of endless one-family houses. At last, a concrete tower with a cross at the top juts up between the houses.

"A church!" Rea shouts, running toward it, and I follow her.

Soaked to the bone, we sit down on a pew in the cold church. Candles flicker on the altar in red plastic votives. There's a Jesus painted on the wall. He hangs, small and fragile, from a golden crucifix. To our left and right great columns of light-colored concrete soar to the ceiling. Rain streams down the high windows.

"This makes me sick," Rea says and shakes her head, sending a spray of fine droplets into my face and onto the floor. "Churches are awful," she says. "You know, at my grandfather's funeral, while everyone was sitting there with their heads bowed, I suddenly started to laugh. Just like that, no reason, and there was nothing I could do about it. That was the worst of it: I couldn't stop myself. It was dreadful, because I really didn't want to laugh. I would rather have been dead, lying in my grandfather's coffin myself, than have to endure the sound of my own laughter and the feeling of all those eyes on me, staring at me in horror. Somebody came and led me out of the church, and I had to wait until the service was over and my parents and relatives came out. I spent the reception chewing on a piece of bread and trying not to look anyone in the eye."

Rea gives a short, cramped chuckle. She's taken off her sunglasses to dry the lenses on her T-shirt.

"Hey, you know what? I'm going to give you my sunglasses!"

I shake my head no.

"Yeah, I will. I'll give them to you and buy myself a new pair—for Milwaukee."

We sit in the church as if it's a cage, and it seems the rain will never stop.

"We could go visit your mother in the hospital before we take off," I suggest to Rea. Suddenly I really want to do it. She shrinks back in surprise. Disgust flashes in her eyes, which I am now seeing for the first time. It flows out to her brow and her mouth, which narrows to a thin strip of flesh, lips sucked in.

"You're fucked in the head, Jo."

THE SCORPIONS have returned from the walls to the ceiling rafters. They won't be back out until next summer. I pull my suitcase out from under the bed and pack up my clothes and books and the postcards I never sent. It's still cool out, this early in the morning, and the letters on the Nova Park Hotel sign sway into sight through the branches of the poplars. But you can already feel the blasting heat that will be here in a couple of hours. Rea has invited me to come stay at her place until we can get a flight to Milwaukee. I set my suitcase down in the dining room and take one last walk around the village wall. As I pass the gate and turn the corner, I spot the elderly couple with their dog. They stroll amongst the trees, stop a while, lean against the railing and look out at the city, blue in the hazy distance. The dog snuffles around at the tree roots and lifts his leg. Suddenly the old lady tugs on the leash and drags the dog across the ground. He howls and the lady grabs him by the ears. She says something that sounds like reprimand, and then, from both sides, they go at the dog. The feet of the old couple land on the dog's body in short, heavy blows. The assault lasts only a few seconds. It's not until they're walking off that it occurs to me to say something. I rush over to them, but then, when I am near enough to breathe their sour breath and see their faces, at once fearful and brutal, I am overcome by revulsion. I keep quiet and walk quickly away.

At the bus station I study the timetables. I have a half an hour to get my things. I try to think about Rea and going to Milwaukee to get the old people out of my head. Back at the house I close up all the drawers and cabinets. I want to get out of here as fast as possible. In the bathroom the bottle of shampoo stands open. While I'm screwing on the lid, the phone rings. Rea's voice whispers into my ear: "Listen, it's gotten really bad with my mother. You can't come now. We have to put off the trip. I'll call you when it's all over, okay?"

F O R T E N days the light blazed down upon me. The pain began in my head and gradually spread to the rest of my body. At first, I went around with my eyes scrunched up when I was out in the garden or shopping in town. Then, when it didn't get better, I put on the sunglasses Rea had given me in the church. The world turned orange and, later on, greenish as waves of nausea crashed through me and I tumbled into bed. I hid under the covers from the rays of light that penetrated the blinds and shone into the room, spreading out across the floor, the table and the bed. I imagined caves, caves that opened up from narrow crevices into vast caverns. I wanted to drag myself in there and roll into a ball, breathing where there was no light, no noise, no panicked existence. During the days I lay on the mattress, soaked through with sweat, and made myself as small as possible. Nights, when I woke up in between dreams and looked out into the darkness, I would allow my feet to protrude from the covers and bask in the cool air, imagining that I lay on the beach with the waves lapping my toes.

Now the screeching from Giuseppe's birds has woken me up. The bed where I lie is an island about to be subsumed by the sea.

The blinds slap against the window frames, and a cool wind blows in from somewhere. Today the rays of sunlight sail faintly, unthreateningly, into the room like well-fed, sleepy falcons. I sit up and swing my feet to the floor. The far wall veers toward me and appears to collapse and fall away. As I stare at the legs of the chair, they vanish from the bottom up and are replaced by emptiness, so that the seat seems to be holding itself up independently. The cold of the stone floor penetrates the soles of my feet. Behind me lie the covers, thrown back but still warm, the ruptured chrysalis I have just crawled out of. With every movement my bones crack and grind as if I were already old and decrepit. In my collapsed shell of a body, I am propelled forward, down the steps, through Alois's empty library and the hall to the kitchen, all quite automatically, as if I were being pulled by an invisible string.

I find myself in the bathroom and peer into the mirror. I'm wearing a nightgown of Lucy's that's much too big. The arms hang down along my body like sails. My hair sticks out from my head as if I'd been out in the wind too long, and my lips have dried up into two brittle, sand-colored strips. I lie in the warm water of the bathtub and watch steam rise to the ceiling. I imagine my dead body lying in the morgue on a high autopsy table. The room is very clean, with great chrome basins and white-tiled walls. A man in green scrubs positions my body at the center of the table. Another one lays the metal instruments out in a row. The first man bends quickly over my abdomen, right where the belly button is and, to its right, the brown birthmark. Whenever I look at my body, I see my birthmark, round and brown and slightly raised. I like to look at it. Actually, I'm rather proud of it—not everybody has one, right there next to their belly button. The first man calls the second one over to look, and they lean their heads together and say a few words. I can't make them out, but I understand that they're sharing some filthy joke. Both of them laugh with their heads thrown back. That's the last image. It's clear and it grows increasingly vivid until it is etched on the inside of my skull. I climb out of the tub, wishing it were winter so I could wear some-thing warm.

I wait in front of the television for Rea to call. The phone sits on a little table by the window. I catch myself going over to the window and waiting there for the ring, ready to grab up the receiver. In the evenings, now, I leave the door to the dining room open and sleep in the kitchen, in front of the fireplace, so as not to miss her phone call. But the house remains quiet, and the idea of Rea is lost gradually to the simple realities of the telephone, the table, the TV.

I know now she won't be going with me. Maybe she'll die young, after all, but even that isn't my business anymore, and I'll never find out about it. The words *Rea* and *Milwaukee* shrivel up into tiny balls of anxiety. I am stuffed so full of such balls that they stretch and disfigure me, and I am in danger of bursting at the seams on every side. Each and every one of them is an independently functioning organism. They fight with one another constantly, as each of them wants me to itself. The Lucy ball is the biggest. Sometimes it goes away, but it's here now and growing within me, battling against the others.

I have dialed one of the numbers they show over and over again on TV and ordered myself a pocket-sized computer game. That's how I pass the time. When I press START, apartment buildings appear on the screen. Meteorites hurtle through the sky with a terrible sound, heading straight for the apartment buildings. I'm up there on the roof with a rocket launcher, trying to shoot down the meteorites before they reach the city. When three of the apartment buildings have been destroyed, the city is wiped out and the screen blinks GAME OVER. I keep playing until I save the city. Some of the meteorites are fast and some are slow. The slow ones I give just a small, cautious grin, and destroy them every time. The ones I hit vanish with a hiss. I run around on the roof and fire my rockets into the sky.

I WATCHED from the balcony as Father assembled a swing in the courtyard. He called me down, and I sat on the shiny red seat and gripped the yellow plastic ropes with both hands. I leaned back and bent forward, swooping high in the air, my face wet with tears from the wind. Father stood there and laughed and shouted something out to me, but I didn't even see him anymore. Above me were the clouds with their great white backs, and I wanted to clamber over them and ride up to heaven. I thought I could do it, if only I swung hard enough.

I would tell Luciano this daydream, if only he were standing here next to me in the doorway of the bathroom. Looking in the mirror, I powder my face until it looks back at me like a doll's. I'm getting myself ready for Luciano, who waits a few blocks over in his attic room. It's comforting to know that he's simply there, lying in his room, singing into a tin can as if it were a microphone, not caring if anyone hears him do it or not.

I'm going to find him and go off with him. All you really need is to know someone you can take by the hand and go off with. In front of the house, a cold wind is blowing. It's quiet at the square in the village. The people are all either home or in the bar. Afterimages of the long shadows cast by the men who are now hunched at tables in the bar cling to the pavement on the square. I stand there and look between the curtains at the window. One of the Palmisano brothers is talking to the waiter. He's propped up against the bar with his upper body caved in, as if the waiter had let all the air out of him. He speaks in the labored, gasping tones of a drunk. Luciano is nowhere around, and so I continue on in the direction of his house. I expect to hear his gravelly voice coming from up the street at any moment, but when I get to the house, I can't even find his name on the doorbells. The tag for the top apartment has been removed. I look for a while at the white space where his name had been inscribed. Luciano has already moved to the city. Alone. When I go to turn around, I bump into someone who comes rushing around the corner. It's one of the Palmisano brothers. I keep moving.

"Hey—wait! Were you looking for me?"

"No."

"So why are you hanging around here?"

"That's none of your business, is it? Leave me alone."

His nostrils flare and his voice comes high and thin, like it's being forced out of his little mouth.

"You slut!" he calls, still following me, now totally out of breath, since I'm picking up speed. He thrusts his body forward, with considerable difficulty, it seems. "You're a little slut, you know that? You really are. Why don't you just admit it?"

He doesn't stop talking. His double chin is in constant motion, and he gets so close to me that I can hear his wheezy breath. His words seem to be coming up from some deep dungeon and, free at last, they shoot from his mouth to my head like pellets of hot steel. There's a lump in my throat so large I can't swallow. At last, hoping to escape the unbearable noise coming from his mouth, I break into a run. But the lumbering behemoth comes closer and closer. He grabs at my hair, not ripping it out but tugging on it, almost gently, like a child tugging lightly on a bell pull, just enough to hear the sound of the chime. I take a leap, turn so I am facing him and spit on the ground at his feet. He stands stock still and looks in amazement at the little gob of phlegm before him.

"You want to play Jesus at the Easter festival and carry the cross through the town, don't you, Palmisano? That's your big dream? Well, I promise you, a piece of crap like you will never get the part. You couldn't pull it off, not even for a day, get it? No way."

A tremor passes through his body. His eyes widen as if he doesn't understand what I've said. He stands there with his mouth open, a small black hole beneath his nose. His too-long arms dangle from their sockets like plants that have been ripped from their beds. We stand there for a moment, silently staring at each other. I can see the pain in the black disks of his eyes, which gradually seem not to see me anymore but in which I begin to think I can make out my own reflection.

As I pass the church, I nearly step on a cat lying on a section of carpet. She rises, purring loudly, and follows me down the street. Her pregnant stomach is tight, like she's ready to have her kittens any moment, and swings from side to side beneath her as she moves. She turns into an alleyway with me, then vanishes into a hole in a cellar wall.

The sleeping bag is a long dark tube, and I creep into it. Winter has entered the house through the cracks in the walls. Inside the tube, it is totally dark and I can hear the pounding of my pulse in my ears. I would like to fall so deeply asleep that I died in this cocoon, warmed at the end only by the beating of my heart and the ebb and flow of my breath.

A quiet, incessant snowstorm dominates my dreams tonight. A cat appears, giving birth to her young in a cellar. The snow is falling, even in there, and it covers her. Then, steps approach quickly from far away. I can't see anything but this white curtain of snowflakes, and the only sound is the crunching of shoes that belong to some invisible, threatening person. In the morning the fabric of Lucy's nightgown sticks to my skin. I get up and go out to the garden, leaving damp impressions of my bare feet on the cold stone floor as I go. They last only a moment. The earth in the garden is dry and cracked. The trunk of the fig tree juts from the hard ground like a bone. Small, shrunken fruits hang from its branches. All the flowers are withered and brown. The air smells like snow. The sheet that Lucy once lay on is still lying there on the floor in the pollen room. I remember a smell that used to hang in the air of this room, but the cold has banished all smells for the time being. Alois no longer peers out from the corners. The walls are smooth and damp. The house is the way it was before he and Lucy moved in. There is nothing left to recall their presence. Even the pollen lies on the floor like a golden carpet, as if it had never been collected and brought here by her hands but had drifted in on its own over the years through the open windows. The room makes it seem that there is no other world outside it, no houses, no rooms, no people to live in them. This house and its garden are paralyzed by the cold air, awaiting the first snow.

It doesn't feel like a departure, as the bus descends the hill. I have not locked or shut the door to the house. Perhaps, when winter comes, stray cats will wander in. They will crouch together on my bed, a great ball of warm, breathing fur while outside winter rages. I left what food there was in the house out on the kitchen table, but some of the cats will starve to death anyhow.

The train station in this town is so small that most of the trains on the line pass it by. I pace back and forth in front of the station, waiting for my train. The shopping center across the way is closed. No one's in sight on the square. The shopping center, like everything, looks dingy in the gray light. Only the construction workers ripping up the street in front of the station stand out in their yellow jumpsuits. Further up, the street has been blocked off, and despite the attempts of policemen to divert the crowded lanes of traffic, impatient motorists nose ever closer to the barricade with their bumpers, as if they simply can't believe that they won't be permitted to travel through. On the other side of the street is a café, and through the plate-glass window, silhouettes are visible of people sitting and reading newspapers. They seem completely unaware of the incredible traffic jam taking place a few yards away. I envy the people who can just walk in there, order coffee, cross their legs and flip through the news. They don't even give the window a glance, as if the street didn't exist or at any rate had no importance. Between the café and where I stand lies the construction site. To get across, I'd have to go all the way to the end of the block and back down, but I don't have that much time left before my train comes. One of the construction workers is shoveling gravel. It's Luciano, dressed just like the rest of them in yellow coveralls. His forehead runs with sweat. I call out to him and wave good-bye, but no matter how loud I yell, he doesn't raise his head. The din is too great for me to overcome. Suddenly he stops working, tosses the shovel aside and sits down. Staring blankly in front of him with his mouth agape, his hands on his knees, he looks like a small endangered animal that is too exhausted even to seek shelter.

T H E   T R A I N I board is silver-white with a long, narrow snout. I find an empty center seat in a six-person compartment. I am wedged in between two passengers, both of whom have taken full possession of the shared armrests. It is a remarkable feeling to sit in such close contact with perfect strangers. Everyone else in the compartment is reading, but since I have no book that I can use as a shield to hide behind, I lean forward slightly so I can look out the window at the scenery. There is no draft of air from the window, no rattling

sound of train wheels. Even when a train whizzes
past in the opposite direction, there is not the slight-
est disturbance. In this vacuum that slides across a
railway line, I cross the border. A woman comes to
the doorway, legs straddled wide. She is there to
check our passports. Her gaze sweeps palpably
across our faces, though no one looks up to meet it.
The others put down their books and newspapers,
and a general rustling in bags and jacket pockets
ensues. Each person in this compartment seems to
fear being suspected of some grave crime. The girl
across from me bends down to the ground over her
bag and her belly rolls over her belt, which is far
too tight for her. She is trying to look casual, but
the quiver at the corner of her mouth betrays her
fear. The door has hardly shut again when all the
books and papers are lifted up in front of the faces
once again. I can't stop thinking about the appearance of the customs officer, and wonder if she will
perhaps return and throw me off the train. It's happened before. People have been locked up unjustly
because they were mistaken for others. The girl
with the tight belt is reading a magazine called
Lisa. The woman on the cover smiles at me. She
seems to whisper at me: But why should anyone
mistake you in particular for someone else? That's
ridiculous. There are so many people on this train.
And you sit here and worry about it. You're too
scared even to lift up your elbow and set it on the

armrest. You have that right, at least. Everyone gets one armrest. Don't you get it? Everyone.

The girl closes the magazine wearily. *Lisa* lies folded in her lap. I do not understand how a person can fall asleep when someone else is sitting right across from them with wide-open eyes. She's got herself straight in the chair, leaning back against the headrest as if she's propped up by cotton wadding. She looks so comfortable that it drives me crazy. I hope she has nightmares that wake her screaming from her nap. She'll scream so loud the others jump in their seats and then offer her consolation. One will even go so far as to fetch her a glass of water. The girl will be terribly embarrassed, she'll apologize and touch her face and hair fretfully and, in an attack of nervousness, root around for the powder compact in her bag. In the midst of this disturbance I'll remain seated, nod at her in a friendly, understanding way, and, as if it were the most natural thing in the world, put *both* my elbows on the armrest. I once read that you can influence people's actions by focusing all your mental energy and concentrating on what you want them to do. I picture the girl's sleep as a spinning top into which I implant dreams that spiral out of control and go wild in every possible way, gradually robbing her of any rest. Her eyelids show not the faintest flicker of motion.

In the great waiting room at the station, I stop

to look for Father's letter with his new phone number. I rummage around in my suitcase for some time while, all around me, people run for trains. Just off to one side, a group of kids has gathered. They're setting off on a class trip and shout out strange, indecipherable phrases to one another, though they're standing so close together they could whisper if they wanted to. One boy passes around a box of chocolate cookies. They devour them in short order, look around sheepishly and, suddenly panicked that they'll miss the train, run all at once into the stream of travelers heading for the platforms.

The people here don't look any different from the ones in the town I left this morning. Their voices have the same sound, and Rea is probably right that it wouldn't be much different in Milwaukee either.

I was expecting Father, but it's Anna who answers and tells me in a sleepy voice that I can't speak with Father just now—he's in bed with a cold. But she'll come pick me up right away. A quarter hour later, I climb into a roomy, dark-green car, a real family car, the kind you can take on vacation. Her belly bulges out from beneath the steering wheel, and I am shocked because I always think of Anna as slim and bony. I look at her stomach again, and it takes me a minute before I realize that she's pregnant.

"Oh my God, you're—I mean, that's—" I can

tell I don't sound very enthusiastic, but she drives along smiling, with her hand resting on top of it.

"Yes. You didn't know about it. I'm in my seventh month."

The first thing I see, when I walk into the house, is a baby carriage standing at the ready in the hallway. Anna leads me up to the top floor, where my father's room is. His face is turned toward the window. It smells of herbal tea and fresh towels in here. On the table by the bed is a bottle of cough syrup and next to it a sticky spot where the spoon must have been set down. It's very warm in the room. Father's eyes are glazed with fever. His skin is dry and somehow scaly. A vaporizer burbles next to the bed.

"I was hoping you'd be back soon. I didn't want to tell you in a letter. They say it's going to be a girl. We saw her for the first time yesterday—on the ultrasound. The doctor said she's completely normal."

As he tells me that I am welcome to stay with them and that Anna will help me to find a job, I look around the room for the cigarette butts that used to collect on the windowsills like little toy soldiers. It disturbs me to see that there are none, somehow much more so than the baby or the calm expression on Father's face. Much more so than the spots on the backs of his hands, which I see now for the first time, and the vaporizer and the depressing burbling that never ceases.

"Did you quit smoking?" My question surprises him so much that he doesn't respond for a moment but smiles at me indulgently, and I have to dig my fingernails into the palms of my hands to keep from punching him in the face. Anna walks into the room without knocking, to take his temperature.

PAULINE LIVES in the cellar. She tells me she had to move out of the upstairs room to make room for the baby. Together we drag a mattress for me down from the loft and put it next to her bed. Pauline's got on a man's shirt and black thigh-highs. She shows me a picture of her boyfriend. He's wearing camouflage battle dress, standing on a field and pointing a machine gun. His jaw juts forward aggressively, impatient to pull the trigger at last. Pauline explains proudly that he's in the army and has already been made an officer. This weekend she's driving up into the mountains with him to take a survival training course. I ask her if she still plays piano, but she just wrinkles up her nose in disgust and begins to grouse about my father and Anna, saying now they'll have something to keep them busy. With her they didn't quite manage it. I don't know what she means but I don't ask. In the corner of her room is an aquarium. Two fish, separated by a glass divider, swim back and forth in synchronized motion. Pauline sits down next to the aquarium with her arms crossed.

"You know what would happen if the divider was removed?" she asks and smiles maliciously. I shake my head.

"They'd eat each other. First kill and then devour. They're just waiting for someone to do it."

When I ask her later exactly why she's going to do survival training, she looks at me uncomprehendingly. Apparently I have just asked the stupidest question she's ever heard. At dinner Anna and Father whisper together like conspirators. Pauline throws the food down her throat and gets up from the table without speaking. I can't stop looking at the mountain of belly that Anna pushes out in front of her, not a heavy one that weighs her down but one filled with air that buoys her up and permits her to open closed doors without knocking.

IT'S DARK in the room. Only the aquarium is illuminated, and the fish swim back and forth without stopping. It almost seems they're eyeing each other. The stray blue tendrils on their backs fan out in alarm, shining like bits of metal in the water. They just keep swimming back and forth across the length of the divider, and I ask Pauline if these damn fish ever lay off and get some rest. Pauline lies next to me but up on the bed with her face turned to the wall. She doesn't respond. She may be sleeping or even crying quietly into the wall for all I know. The walls of this house are so thin you can hear the baby growing. Anna's belly pulsates, and the walls watch over it as if they were built for no other purpose. It's a belly that grows and grows, stuffed so full of things, including even father's cigarette stubs, that it's cramped for space. Suddenly it occurs to me that Father has never asked me about Lucy. He's absolutely avoided bringing the subject up since I came. And if he did, what could I tell him about her whose face has faded in my memory to a washed-out speck with whom it's impossible to hold a conversation? The blue ballet shoes that she bought for me ten years ago and never sent. I cannot imagine anything I detest more than that pair of shoes. Slowly I gather my things together. I leave the shoes on the kitchen table with a note that says, *For her*. In the hallway, where the baby carriage is, I turn around and go back to Pauline's room. I don't look in as I pull the divider from the aquarium. It happens quickly.

In the early morning light, I leave the house. There are no cars out yet, and I walk down the middle of the street, following the white line that divides it in two. I go toward the city this way, as if following a thread that slowly wraps around me with every step I take. From far off I see a light atop a factory smokestack blinking on and off at reliable two-second intervals. Somewhere, there's a room high up in an apartment building where the people sink back in their chairs and let the noise of the city seep away into the walls. I would be able to see the sky from that window, and when I opened it and peered down at the world, everything below would seem as tiny and unthreatening as toys. On the outskirts of town, I come across a park nestled between residential blocks. Blackbirds perch on the bare branches of the trees. The first snow filters down. Two old ladies sit close together on the bench, as stiffly as if they had been stuffed and mounted. They seem to be good and warm, but I've been out a long time in the cold. When I sit down on a bench nearby, they look over at me. There is nothing friendly in their eyes. I know I'm bothering them, but stay where I am nonetheless. I don't tell them that I'm sitting here just to watch the snow fall to earth. This kind of snow doesn't stick at all. It doesn't coat the ground in a layer of pure white, because it melts as soon as it hits the earth, always keeping me waiting for the next flake, for the microsecond when it hits the ground but has not yet melted. I will wait here with the ladies for the snow to coat the ground in a layer of pure white, a white blanket of snow.

Zoë Jenny was born in Basel, Switzerland, in 1974. She grew up in Greece, Tessin and Basel. Since 1993 she has had short stories published in literary journals in Switzerland, Germany and Austria. In August 1997 she published her first novel, *Das Blütenstaubzimmer*, in Germany. She is currently working on a new novel.

Elizabeth Gaffney is an editor at large of *The Paris Review*. She is writing her first novel.

THE POLLEN ROOM

DISCUSSION POINTS

1. Twelve years after her mother disappeared from her life, Jo decides to seek her out. Her feeling of curiosity surprisingly seems mixed with no anger; it's almost apathetic. Do you think it is possible for a daughter to have such a detached attitude toward a parent—particularly a mother?

2. Jo's mother informs her bluntly that they won't talk about the past, that she does not feel "obligated to make amends." How do you view a statement so seemingly devoid of maternal love?

3. At one point, Jo looks for a journal her mother might have kept. What do you think she expects to find? Is she looking for clues about her mother's life? Or for some declaration that somehow her mother hadn't abandoned her—that there was an answer that might give her some peace?

4. Lucy abandoned her daughter as a small child; now, as Jo reaches out to her, Lucy still seems to need to escape. Is Lucy terrified of being responsible for her child? Is she simply self-involved to a pathological degree? How can we reconcile Lucy's behavior with our expectations of motherhood?

5. Unlike Lucy, Jo's father is present—but only tenuously. We can infer from the author's descriptions of Lucy's behavior what her psychological makeup might be. But her father seems more opaque. What kind of man do you think he is?

6. Jo seems alienated from everyone. Is the blame to be placed entirely on her parents? What responsibility does she have for her own emotional life?

7. What emotions did *The Pollen Room* evoke in you? As a mother? As a daughter? Are there any feelings you share with Jo? Would you react as she does in similar situations?

8. Jenny always uses the image of butterflies in *The Pollen Room* in conjunction with death. Could this image suggest Jo's attempts to emerge emotionally but, at the same time, always being thwarted by the reality of her mother's coldness and isolation?

9. "I've been able to escape reality by reading ever since I can remember," says Jo. How many of you share this escape mechanism?

What books have particularly offered escape for you? Are there books you reread often for their ability to take you to another, happier place?

10. Some critics have questioned whether this novel is largely autobiographical. Do you believe that it is the author's own fictionalized story or perhaps her reflections on her generation? How do you see Jo in relation to your experiences at her age?

About the Author

Though not yet thirty years old, Zoë Jenny has already achieved a level of international fame enjoyed by few, engendered by the stunning success of her first novel, *The Pollen Room*. It sold 150,000 copies in Switzerland, making it the most successful debut for a Swiss author in history. Born in Basel, Switzerland, in 1974, she grew up in Greece, Tessin, and Basel. Since 1993 she has had short stories published in literary journals in Switzerland, Germany, and Austria. She is currently working on a new novel.

Discover more reading group guides on-line!
Browse our complete list of guides and download them for free at
www.SimonSays.com/reading_guides.html